Sunny Side Up

Lake Erie Mysteries, Volume 1

Olivia Breen

Published by Olivia Breen, 2021.

Chapter One

The evening sky made me think of rainbow sherbet as I watched the sun set over picturesque Kelleys Island. The sound of waves lapping against the side of my small skiff as I steered toward the lakeshore had a cathartic effect—my breathing and heart rate were finally returning to normal. From a hundred yards off shore, it was a postcard perfect scene. Idling past the breakwall, past the pier and the beach, I watched the fingers of charcoal smoke curl their way through the pastel clouds, clutching and twisting, distorting the idyllic scene. I could almost smell it, faint at first, but increasing in intensity, a foul odor like hot summer asphalt mixed with the sweetly noxious smell of burnt cupcakes. It would make your eyes water and your nostrils burn.

Increasing my speed, I glanced over my shoulder and focused once more on the shoreline, picturing the result of my handiwork and the thrill that would course through me when my mission was complete and my trophy, the charred remains of my victim, was discovered.

Chapter Two

Did I leave my vibrator on? Oh wait, I don't own a vibrator, so what was causing the riotous pile of clothes on my bedroom floor to buzz with such urgency? The mundane truth was that I'd switched my cell phone ringer off so I wouldn't lose focus while trying to assemble my weekend wardrobe. Obviously that wasn't working out so well for me.

I located the gyrating devil under some discarded tank tops and swiped the answer button on the screen right before the call was switched over to voicemail. "Hello?"

"Francie! Is it a go? Did you get the hubby to agree to run us over to the island in the boat this weekend?"

"It's good to hear from you, too, June. And no, I haven't gotten around to asking him yet. He's downstairs whipping up one of his gourmet meals, and I sure don't want to distract him from that. I was trying to figure out what I should pack. How do you prepare for freezing cold mornings, balmy afternoons, torrential downpours and high winds—and fit everything into one suitcase? At least I don't have to worry about bathing suits. After the winter we've just had, the lake probably won't warm up until August."

"Sorry. I'm just anxious to get to the island. My editor is jumping down my throat to get this story in before the official start of the season."

June's passion was hard to resist. She was like that about everything she did—she took off running and didn't look back. I could feel myself being lured in to the promise of fun and adventure. It wouldn't be the first time.

My best friend is a freelance writer. She works for a consortium of specialty magazines running the gamut from Fruit Aficionado to The Neighborhood Cigar, to my favorite—Lady Sings the Tools. Two years ago she gave up her high-profile job as an investigative reporter for WCLV, the major network news channel in Cleveland. After her divorce, she bagged up all her corporate outfits, chopped off her hair, and set off on a new career path that didn't hamper her free spirit. Her new job now requires her to spend time with all kinds of interesting people from every walk of life instead of digging up dirt on the lowest of low-life criminals.

Recently, I even got to meet Christie Browne, the beautiful model, while June was working on a story about the latest beauty product the star was endorsing. In our enthusiasm to prove our support for the much-touted self-tanning lotion, we doubled the recommended amount as well as the recommended usage time. Our skin turned a frightening shade of burnt pumpkin, and wouldn't you know it, I had to accompany my husband Hammond to a formal dinner party given by his firm that same evening. June, on the other hand, was able to postpone her face-to-face interview, and by the time we met Christie, we both looked sweetly sun-kissed. She got rave reviews on her piece. I got put on a prayer list.

"I get that you're under a deadline, but if I don't approach Hamm in just the right way, I'm fried. Let me call you back."

"Okay, but let me know soon. If I don't take this assignment, I'll be stuck documenting the mating behaviors of ferrets for the next two weeks."

"Don't worry. I'll call ya back. I promise."

"Okay, but..."

I clicked off the call, tucked my cell phone into the back pocket of my favorite worn jeans, and hustled down the stairs to the kitchen.

"Seriously, Francesca? Was that June again?"

"What? I wasn't talking to anyone. I was just sorting through my closet to see what I would need in case we headed up to the lake for the weekend."

"You know you can't just pack up and take off after that nut job friend of yours every time she goes off on one of her top-secret missions or assignments or whatever the heck they are. The university doesn't appreciate you turning up AWOL whenever Miss Batman sends up her rally signal."

My husband had a point. I selected a bottle of Pinot Noir and poured two glasses while trying to judge his mood.

Hamm is logical, thoughtful, intelligent, and often introspective. I, on the other hand, live in the moment, embracing the passions of the people around me. Although Hamm was speaking sternly, he wasn't fooling me. He was having a hard time suppressing the smile turning up the corners of his mouth and making the emerging crow's feet around his eyes crinkle.

"Hamm, you know the semester is over, and I'm finished with the drama department for the summer. There's nothing but sunshine and blue skies in my immediate future."

The guy just didn't have it in him when he knew a battle was not to be won. He shook his head, turned his back to me and focused his attention once more on the cast iron pan he wielded over the front burner of our commercial-grade stove. The fact Hammond loves to cook and is proficient at it makes loving him easy.

At the moment, he was scurrying around the kitchen, putting together one of his traditional Norwegian recipes, a bacon and egg cake. The main ingredients of this heavenly meal consists of three-quarters of a pound of crisp bacon, six eggs, two-thirds cup of half-and-half, and a few secret herbs. He liked to personalize his version with a generous portion of Jarlsberg cheese. There is no such thing as a half-cup serving of this recipe, and this is why I'm a life-long member of Weight Watchers.

I flashed a big smile his way when he turned to ask me for the pepper shaker. "I love you, honey, but you know darn well I won't be changing my ways any time soon."

"Oh, don't I know. The food is ready. Let's eat before it gets cold."

Perfect timing, I thought. All of that packing had made me hungry. I admit I've been spoiled by my husband over the last twenty-two years. I picked up my glass of wine, silently toasted my best friend, and took my seat at our barn-plank kitchen table. Its old-fashioned, wax pine patina blended well with our whitewashed, clean-lined kitchen chairs.

A heaping portion of bacon and egg cake was already served up and waiting for me. Hamm filled his plate at the counter and took his spot across from me. We sat for a while in companionable silence, savoring each mouthful of the bacony, cheesy dish. Finally, I placed my fork on my placemat, wiped the corners of my mouth, and cleared my throat. It was time to put my plan into action.

"Dinner was out of this world, hon. I'll clear the table and do the dishes if you'll just hear me out for a minute. By the time I'm finished, I bet you'll be grabbing your keys and pulling me out the front door."

Hamm stared across the table at me with a look of resignation on his handsome face.

"We're talking about the same thing, right? You are referring to that spiky-haired, skinny journalist friend of yours who just blurts out her every thought and opinion without benefit of a social filter? I cringe every time she opens her mouth."

I sent my best flirty eyelashes in his direction. "Yeah, yeah, of course, Hamm. But you love me, right? You know June likes to have company when she has to stay overnight to do research for one of her articles. Humor me for a minute." Another eyelash bat. "Contrary to popular belief, her super powers don't always include the desire to be a one-woman show, especially since her split with Cliff. Sometimes she's downright shy."

"Hmmph." It was the best he would give me for the time being. At least he didn't offer to get me some eye drops.

His silent treatment let me know he was giving some thought to what I said. Looking every bit like he might regret his next words, he replied. "Okay, let's have it. What's this latest adventure? I guess it can't be any worse than last winter when the two of you got so caught up in the daily life of a mall security guard you ended up locked inside Macy's overnight. You're lucky you weren't arrested."

"Well, you don't have to keep bringing that up. First of all, you'll like the setting of her latest assignment. June's been commissioned to research and write an article about the many offerings on Kelleys Island for the romantic and adventurous. Her boss wants her to visit the stores and boutiques on the island and see what different kinds of merchandise are available to spice up adult play time, if you know what I mean."

"Who's going to read a story on that? You wouldn't think there would be much available on the island in the first place. But then again, what would I possibly know about that?"

"Oh, you'd be surprised. Believe it or not, there's a lot of interest in toys and such for grown-ups, and retailers are always looking for ways to stimulate the...eh hem...economy."

Hamm sucked in air and choked on his wine. It's not like I was asking him to perform some kinky sex act on the kitchen table. Hmmm. Then again... I mentally slapped myself and brought my attention back to the real-life conversation.

"June's boss got a lead on some creative new lines being sold, and apparently, the boutiques on the island want in on the action. She wants her to get the scoop before the summer season gets into full swing. I can't wait to see what all the buzz is about. She says that Ruby's Treasure Chest has expanded, and the shop now has a section in the back for her twenty-one and over clients."

The face of my conservative lawyer husband had just turned a shocking shade of red.

"Oh, I can hardly wait."

"There's no need for sarcasm just because you aren't interested in the fascinating world of retail. Think about this for a minute. Memorial Day means we could have a nice three-day weekend. It's just a six-mile boat ride to the island from the condo, the winds are going to be calm, the weather forecast is calling for seventy-six degrees and sunny, and the first pitcher of Brandy Alexanders at the Village Pump is calling your name!"

"Well, there is that."

Hammond ran his long fingers through his thick, dark hair. I thought the recent glint of silver at his temples made him look a little like George Clooney. I also thought that it was damn unfair that my husband got sexier as he got older while I just spent more and more time and money chasing the elusive fountain of youth. At least my shoulder-length, dark curls were still bouncy, and with the right styling products and a little effort, I could still pull off a passable version of "youthful chic." I'm not embarrassed to admit I have a flair for putting together some attention-getting fashion looks; I can find my way around a thrift shop or Nordstroms with equal success.

Hammond blew out a sigh. "Okay. I guess you're right. There's a full tank of gas in the boat, and I would enjoy a trip out to Kelleys to kick off the season. But does she have to stay with us at the condo? And just so we're clear, she's not staying on the boat too when we get there. It would be nice to relax and enjoy the weekend without an agenda, but whenever June's around, chaos is a given."

"Hamm, give June a break. For your information, her houseboat is already at the dock. She had the water and electrical systems inspected, and the marina manager gave her the green light to stay aboard. She has the galley stocked with provisions and is ready to call Anchor Management her floating cottage for the summer."

"Well, there is that."

I knew I had him hooked. The thought of our first long weekend at the lake, warm breezes, sunny skies, and for the most part, June-free condo living was more than my dear husband could resist.

I hummed a show tune as I cleared our plates and loaded the dishwasher. I didn't have to worry about packing up leftovers. Once again, there weren't any. When I had finished tidying up in the kitchen, I went to my favorite spot in the family room. The soft mahogany leather of the L-shaped sofa was wrinkled and dipped in just the right places. I stretched out my legs, checked my toenails for chipped polish, and retrieved my cell phone from my pocket. June picked up on the very first ring.

"We're in!" I announced. "I'm packed and I can't wait to get started. What luck that your latest job wasn't writing about computer classes for pets. I'm highly allergic to cats you know."

"I didn't think you'd mind being my unpaid research assistant on this one. I am curious though. What did you have to promise Hamm to get him to agree?

"Nothing much," I replied.

Chapter Three

Early Friday morning, we loaded up Hammond's shiny black SUV and hit the road, making one quick stop at Starbucks for a couple steaming black coffees. As the city faded away in the rearview mirror, my mind drifted back to the late spring day seventeen years ago when our love affair with Ohio's north shore began.

"I'm home, Francie. You look gorgeous, sweetheart. Is that a new outfit?"

He bent down and kissed me on the top of my head—the only portion of me he could find not covered in sweet potatoes and applesauce. I loved how he always complimented me even when I knew he had to pull out all of his lawyer tricks to keep a straight face.

"How are my little bumble bees?" Hamm swept our daughter, Beth, up in a big bear hug, ignoring the addition of orange goo from her adoring little face to his emerging five o'clock shadow. He gave her a twirl then set her gently down on the vinyl kitchen floor. Next he directed his attention to her twin brother, Ben, tickling him under his chubby arms. Ben squealed in delight, grabbed Hamm around the knees and stomped on his foot. It's a good thing his darling son had pulled off his shoes and socks and launched them across the kitchen just a minute before his daddy arrived home from work. After their exuberant welcome home antics, the two-year-olds giggled and went right back to babbling on in the private language only twins comprehended.

"The coffee smells like heaven, Francie. I don't know how you always manage to have a fresh pot on the counter when I walk through the door."

"It might be my only carry-over skill from my former life," I replied sweetly as I got up to pour him a cup.

After high school, I thought I wanted a career in law enforcement and was working as an intern to the Cleveland prosecuting attorney when I met the handsome law clerk destined to become the father of my children. Coffee making and serving was one of the very first skills I had mastered for my demanding boss. Over the years, I transitioned from my dreams of being an undercover sleuth to the satisfying reality of wife, mother, and eventually PhD in English and Drama. Now I got to take on alternate personas without risking my life. As far as I was concerned, I had it all.

Hammond loosened the yellow silk tie I had recently scored from the clearance bin at Macy's. Even as a young mother, I'd always had an eye for fashion, a nose for a bargain, and a knack for dressing on a dime.

Settling into the red, vinyl-covered chair across from me, a smile spread across Hamm's handsome face and lit up the tiny kitchen of our two-bedroom suburban bungalow.

"Spill it, darling! And I don't mean the coffee."

The goofy grin on his face was not a typical expression for my serious husband. I could tell Hamm had something he was itching to tell me.

Clearing his throat, Hamm began three times before he finally got it out. "Honey, umm, I, uh, I sort of put a small down payment on a used boat. Would you like to come with me to the dealer tomorrow and take a look before we finalize the deal?"

I gathered my wits, shut my gaping pie hole, took a deep breath, and said, "Are you sure about this? Can we afford it? Are the twins too young? Can you even drive a boat?"

"Yes. Maybe. No. And we're about to find out."

It took less than a week to become the proud owners of our first floating weekend home. The boat was small and light and didn't handle well in rough water, but what did we know? We were boaters now and about to make the first of hundreds of this very same drive to the perfect weekend spot for affordable family fun.

My thoughts came back to the present as we rolled up to the gate of Beacon Pointe Resort. The middle-aged guard in the gatehouse put on his glasses, adjusted the brim of his floppy hat, and inspected our residence sticker on the windshield. "Welcome back, Mr. and Mrs. Egge. Hope you had a good winter."

"Thanks, Steve. The winter was uneventful, cold, and way too long, just like every year."

I leaned across the seat and added, "We're just excited to be back to our happy place!"

The guard raised the gate-arm and waved us into the resort. The speed limit was ten miles per hour, just like it had been for over fifteen years. Children laughed and squealed on the swing set as we drove past the park. I remembered how my own kids had spent hours doing the same things, running and playing until dark when they were forced to come in, eat something, and crash, too tired to protest, just to wake up early and do it all again the next day.

Fit, young athletes with earbuds and iPods checked their times as they jogged around the walking path. A couple, well into their eighties by the looks of them, strolled hand-in-hand along the same route. Geese honked and pooped everywhere. Some things never change.

We pulled up to the cedar and stone condominium we now called our second home. Fuchsia geraniums in white clay pots stood sentry on the front porch complementing the cream window trim and rich rose-colored front door. I stepped slowly out of the passenger door. Practicing a few yoga moves, I managed to loosen up the muscles in my back and legs that had tightened from spending over an hour in the car. I made my way out toward the backyard. Tall seagrass framed the restful view of the gray blue lake, and I inhaled deeply. Lucky for me, the breeze was out of the south, so I smelled blossoms and fresh air instead of dead fish. Off in the distance, boats dotted the water. Some were pulling water-skiers, others hauled kids in tubes, and there was one brave soul floating in the air above a boat with a parasailing logo emblazoned on its hull.

Entering the condo through the back door, I noticed the faint scent of lemon polish emanating from the entry hall. Anna, our seasonal cleaning lady, had been here this morning. Gold flecks in the kitchen's granite island sparkled in the afternoon sun. Real lemons and limes filled a glass bowl on the counter adding to the sheer citrusy pleasure of the room. I tossed my bag into our bedroom and returned to the kitchen to perform my seasonal ritual of opening and closing all the cupboards and drawers, reacquainting myself with the whereabouts of the day-to-day trappings of what I now thought of as my "real life."

I noticed the bottle of wine Hamm had set out for me. I truly am spoiled. I'm by no means a wine connoisseur, but I have a few small quirks that make my drinking ritual special. I especially enjoy the gurgly, whiny song the red wine sings as it passes through the aerator into my awaiting stemware. I poured a small glass and made my way outside to the patio where Hammond was lounging in the sun, admiring the golden glow of his Jack Daniels on the rocks. He was about to light his first cigar of the season when the expression on his face turned stormy.

I followed his stare upward to the dark shadow descending over our patio. Some lunatic had actually released that parasailer, and the wayward adventurer was making a landing right on the beach behind our condo. The person touched down in the sand, forward momentum pushing both parachute and rider smack into the middle of the petunia bed that edged our patio. Hammond and I sprung out of our chairs and took cover in the doorway. Puffs of wind billowed out from the collapsing purple- and green-striped parachute while the daredevil it had carried thrashed around, struggling to get free. From beneath the folds of the tangled sail, a familiar voice sounded out.

"Hi, Doc! How's it crackin' Egg?"

June had arrived.

From the relative safety of the doorway, I stared at my windblown friend as she extricated herself from the silky fabric. Considering she had just fallen from the sky, she was remarkably calm and collected. She looked like a superhero stopping by to say hello, and I easily imagined her leaping back up into the blue and flying off to save the world from mayhem. Hamm was more likely imagining her disappearing as he completed his "Woe is me. What did I ever do to deserve this?" eye roll and sigh.

It was obvious June's juvenile greeting was not appreciated by my husband. Hammond Egge, Esquire is most definitely not an egg. His paternal ancestors hailed from Norway, by way of Bird Island, Minnesota. His family name, Egge, rhymes with ledge, but much to the chagrin of his entire family, most everyone finds it exceedingly amusing to make clever references to omelets, shells, and Mother Goose nursery rhyme characters when talking to him. June's silly nicknames never bothered me though, since I hung on to my maiden name. Dr. Francesca Orsini gets respect. Francie Egge, not so much.

"Looks like I'm in time for cocktails. Are there snacks? I'm starving." After flashing my husband her model-worthy smile, June strolled right past us into the kitchen, poured herself a generous glass of my wine, and began rummaging through the cupboards and fridge in search of snacks.

"I guess some sort of cheese plate will do."

Hamm was looking at me in absolute disbelief. "Francie, I'm assuming I dozed off while waiting for you to unpack because I know it can't be true that your nutty friend landed her parachute in our backyard and strolled into our kitchen to prepare snacks. Wake me up when the planet begins spinning the right way."

"I'm confident the Earth is still rotating on its axis, honey. I guess June didn't have cab fare. Don't be upset. At least she's pitching in and preparing some food."

"Seriously, Francesca? Hamm glared through the French doors and exhaled. "Well, there is that."

When June reappeared on the deck, she was carrying a five-star presentation of hors d' oeuvres: Gouda and Swiss wedges alongside sesame and whole grain crackers artfully arranged on an artisan platter I didn't realize I owned. This was one of the reasons I loved June. She has a flair for the dramatic and a talent for improvisation that rivals even the best stage actress. She does especially well with other people's belongings.

"So, June, that was quite the arrival. What's up with the parachute? Was there road construction or something?" I was dying to hear this story.

Hamm chose to stare at his plate and munch his snacks in silence while June explained.

"I called a cab right after I talked to you last night. Traffic was light and we made excellent time. After I unpacked my stuff at the houseboat, I decided to take a ride on the shuttle boat across the bay to Sandusky and get a bite to eat at Famous Dave's. I met the nicest guy while I was waiting for a table."

"Well now, there's a surprise." I couldn't help it.

"He has a new parasail business and offered to take me for a ride. I had such a good time I decided to go back today and practice some moves. Marley agreed to take me across the bay so I could surprise you guys. Did it work?"

"I would say so. I thought Wonder Woman was stopping by for tea. Would you like a refill on your drink?"

She peeked in her glass and stretched her arm across the table so I could top off her glass.

Hamm's eyes were now closed as he listened to music streaming from his smartphone. As I sipped my drink and basked in the warmth of the afternoon sun, I admired the purple streak in June's ultra-short hair, wondering where she found the time to coordinate her hair color with her outfits. June, as usual, was ready to move on.

"So when are we leaving for the island? I have to stop at the houseboat to take care of a few things. I can get there and back in thirty minutes. Or better yet, I'll meet you at your boat dock." She popped out of her chair like Beth's old jack-in-the-box and bounced through the house and out the front door.

"Did I miss something?" Hamm asked sleepily.

"June left."

"But?"

"But what? There's no but. I was just thinking. It's going to be such a beautiful evening. There's no wind and the lake looks like glass. Wouldn't you love to hop in the boat and run it over to Kelleys tonight? Then tomorrow morning we can wake up and start our long weekend on the island bright and early."

"That actually sounds good to me. I'll help you clean up."

"By the way, dear, June is meeting us at the dock."

Chapter Four

I grabbed our getaway weekend bag with the few essentials that weren't already on board, and Hamm took charge of my suitcase. "I'm not going to ask what you have in this thing. I'm just glad it has wheels."

We locked the front door and headed up the path toward the boat docks. The marina section of Beacon Pointe was a short walk from the residential district. Some folks liked to ride in their complimentary golf carts, but we preferred to cover the quarter mile or so on foot.

When we arrived at the boat, Hamm stood for a second and took it all in with pride. "You know, hon, no matter how many times we've done this, it still always feels like we're coming home."

"I know exactly what you mean. I feel the same way."

Hamm and I were both looking forward to our first excursion of the season. I was dreaming of fried fish and new flip flops, and I suspected Hamm was envisioning a long, tall drink and that cigar he never got around to finishing. As luck would have it, all these things would have to wait.

True to her word, within moments, June was hauling her backpack over the side of the boat and stepping onto the swim platform in new lime green and purple plaid boat shoes. Her camera case was slung around her neck, and the outline of her cell phone was clearly defined through the back pocket of her skinny purple jeans.

"Hey, lovebirds! Let's get this show on the road."

June's voice had the effect of a rusty nail scraping across the paint job of a brand new Porsche. Hamm winced. June was oblivious. I was happy to be with my two favorite people.

Before Hammond could hyperventilate over the thought of June staying with us on the boat for three days and four nights, she reached into her chirping back pocket and pulled out her iPhone.

"Oh, good! Yes. Thank you so much. I'll be checking in tonight and staying until Tuesday."

June's expression took on a mischievous look. There was a twinkle in her eye. "Yes, that's correct. The credit card is registered to 'Sea What's Sexy.' What? No! I am a writer. A professional! Well, never mind about that. I'll see you shortly."

June smiled as she wriggled her phone back into its snug resting place. "My boss reserved a room for me at the bed and breakfast right next to Ruby's Treasure Chest, so as soon as we get to the island, I can check in, and you and I can walk over and see what's new at her shop."

I was thrilled with the plan. I was also certain that even though Hamm was celebrating in his head after learning that June would be bunking nearby but in private quarters, he was at the same time fervently praying to every saint he could remember from his days in Catholic school that Ruby's fabulous island gift store would be locked up tighter than Davy

Jones' locker by the time we got to the island. He hated shopping. In fact, he feared it.

June and I untied the boat lines and battened down the hatches. I must admit, I make a great first mate and June can hold her own as a deckhand. Once everything was in order, Captain Hammond took his place at the wheel. He looked at his watch for about the tenth time in ten minutes, and I wasn't sure if he was anxious to get underway or making sure he took long enough for Ruby's store to be closed when we got to the island. I sat in my usual spot in the corner of the wraparound bench seat, facing the rear so I could look out at the water and the wake and feel the warmth of the sun on my outstretched legs. The engines were warming up and Hamm was just about to put the boat in reverse when June stood suddenly and put her hands on her hips.

"Wait! We need to make a toast to our first boat ride of the year. I'll be right back."

In a voice worthy of any sea captain, Hamm countered, "You will not be drinking red wine in my boat! The last time you tried that, I was explaining all summer why I changed the deck carpet from tan to pink. I finally got the stains out, so no wine for you! Why do you think that floor mat is right under the spot where you like to sit?"

"Fine. A quick beer then? It's just not right without a toast."

"CHEERS!" WE CLINKED our bottles and toasted to a warm, sunny summer filled with good friends and new memories. Moments later, we were underway. Calm seas and the low, deep thrumming of the dual engines settled all three of us into a state of relaxed reverie. There was something special, too, about the smell of the fresh air, and the way the breeze ruffled my hair. It was funny how my thick, wavy hair always looked better after a boat ride than after an hour in front of the mirror with curling iron and hair spray.

I leaned my head back and closed my eyes; all was well in the world. I was about to give in to the lure of sleep when I found myself struggling against gravity to stay upright in my seat. I looked toward June who was gripping the back of the boat seat with both hands. The long-necked beer bottle she had set on the table was now rolling around the cockpit floor leaving an amber trail of liquid in its path.

"Hamm, what the heck?" I couldn't get his attention. He was clutching the steering wheel and maneuvering the boat into a steep turn. We were bumping and crashing over our own wake, and my teeth were rattling in my head.

"Hey, that wasn't funny! And it's not my fault that I spilled my beer." June was trying her best to retrieve the travelling bottle with her bare feet, but it escaped her wiggling toes and continued on its wild course.

"I'm sorry, girls. Hold on. Some nut in a speed boat is riding up on our tail. He's heading straight for us, and it's a miracle we haven't had a collision. I'm going to slow down now and hope he passes us. Then I'm calling the Coast Guard and reporting this menace."

"Oh geez, some people shouldn't be allowed to operate a watercraft." I straightened up in my seat and finally got a look at the fast-approaching vessel.

"Ouch!" Something crashed into my foot, and I noticed that my empty beer bottle had joined June's in its race around the cockpit. I sure hoped they didn't break because Hamm was always harping on me to drink out of aluminum cans. Yuck. The zippy little speed boat that was causing all the commotion had adjusted its course to match Hamm's new position and was once again heading straight for us.

"I've had just about enough of this maniac." Hamm maneuvered the shifters into neutral and jumped out of his captain's chair to stand up and be seen. June was perched on her knees pointing her camera in our annoying visitor's direction. No doubt she thought this would be a great action shot if the incompetent boater dared to come any closer. It was becoming difficult for me to stave off impending nausea since the smooth ride across the lake had become a bobbing and dipping float. What a way to get our vacation started.

Now that we were no longer moving, I could see the pilot of the boat more clearly. He was looking directly at us, frantically waving his hands in the air, and still heading in a straight line for our starboard beam. At least he had slowed down. Maybe now the hole he was about to punch into the side of the boat wouldn't cause us to sink quite so fast. Hamm stood with his feet planted wide apart and his hands on his hips as the man pulled up alongside us. I was having crazy thoughts about pirates and boat-jackers and was still concentrating on not throwing up. My slow, deep breaths weren't working so well. I hyperventilated a little bit. June, on the other hand, sprung out of her seat and ran to the deck to stand in plain sight of the uninvited guest.

A huge grin spread across her face and she began waving and calling out, "Ahoy there, Marley!"

The smaller craft came to a full stop next to us, and I could now see the parasailing logo and phone numbers emblazoned on the hull and transom of the boat. Uh-oh, this wasn't going to go over well with my husband.

June lost no time engaging in a spirited conversation with Marley, who was the color of my morning java, shirtless, and sporting some wicked dreadlocks. I could see why June struck up such an easy friendship with the guy last night and returned this morning for a second round of lessons with him. I couldn't exactly hear what they were saying, and I didn't want to attract attention to myself by moving in on them, so I sat very still and concentrated on my breathing.

Hamm snuck up behind me and hissed in my ear, "What is your friend's problem?" And to make certain there was no mistake about his feelings, he added the death glare he reserved for just such occasions.

Apparently, Marley wanted his parachute back and had been on his way to the condo to pick it up when he noticed us leaving. He had a pair of college girls scheduled for a lesson in an hour and he didn't have June's cell phone number, so he followed us.

June apologized for being scatterbrained and explained where she had left his chute. And as quick as that, Marley revved his engine and took off back in the direction from where we had come. As soon as our path was clear, Hamm resumed his role of captain. He slammed the shifters into the forward position, throttled up, and pointed us back on course for our destination. I decided it was probably best if we remained low-key for the rest of our short trip. I picked up the empty but unbroken beer bottles and made a mental note to wipe down the fiberglass floor when we got to the dock, glad to see the carpet was not wet or stained. June plopped down on the seat, looking contrite and mouthing "sorry" in my direction. I gave her a thumbs-up and she responded with her best June grin.

Before we knew it, we could see the distinctive blue roof of Seaway Marina, the safest harbor on Kelleys Island. Hammond slowed the boat and eased into our assigned dock like the experienced skipper he was, and I hopped into action, determined to recover the light mood we had at the onset of our trip. Making my way to the bow of the boat, I had lines and fenders at the ready.

"Ahoy, mates. How was your winter?" Alex, the handsome, young dock hand, called out as he effortlessly caught the lines I tossed and secured them to the dock cleats.

"We're happy to be back. What's new and exciting on the island for this season?"

"Well, there's a new chef over at West Bay Inn. Be sure to take a ride over there. You won't be sorry. Oh, and there's a new store you and your friend would probably like. I can't remember the name of the place, but you can't miss it. There's a giant mermaid in the front yard."

"A mermaid? Did you hear that, June? That sounds interesting."

"Maybe that's one of the new boutiques I need to check out for my magazine article. Sounds good."

Hammond groaned. "Oh greaaaat."

I smiled like the Cheshire cat as I looked up from the neatly tied nautical knot I had executed to see the lovely red door of Ruby's Treasure Chest glowing across the way beneath the brightly-lit "Open" sign.

Chapter Five

There was still plenty of daylight left when we arrived, but my internal dinner bell was indicating it was close to mealtime. "Who's up for pizza at Caddy Shack?" I couldn't help it. I hadn't even finished unpacking my bag, but I had a sudden urge for the local restaurant's signature white pizza. They did amazing things with spinach, tomatoes, feta cheese, olive oil, and pistachio nuts.

Hamm was busy unfolding our marine bicycles that had been stashed in the aft cabin during the ride over. "Let me get this finished up here and we'll go. I'm pretty hungry too, and their mushroom and onion pizza is delicious."

"Hey, June!" I started to ask her what she was in the mood for, but before I got out my next sentence, I saw her standing on the grass, facing the parking lot and the street beyond. She was already at work, snapping photos of Ruby's boutique with her zoom lens. In spite of her unconventional appearance, June was focused and professional when it came to her job. When she heard the mention of food, however, it was all over.

"Sausage, ground beef, pepperoni, and ham for me!" called June over her shoulder. "I'm ready!"

Sometimes I was the teeniest bit jealous of my friend's ability to consume mass quantities of food and never add an ounce to her lithe frame. She was built like a ballerina and had the stamina of a marathon runner despite the fact I had never seen her do a pirouette or lace up a pair of serious running shoes. I, on the other hand, had to be constantly vigilant to maintain my size-eight figure. Three summers ago, while on this very island, I was forced to head over to the Village Peddler to purchase a pair of shorts with "emergency elastic." That fall, I joined Weight Watchers and the local gym and vowed never to return to that state of affairs again. I did miss eating cheese and chips with utter abandon sometimes, but I much prefer the way my new and improved fit and curvy figure looked and felt in my clothes.

Watching Hamm and June, I felt like I was the only one being unproductive, so I went back to the job of unpacking my suitcase. I hung all my clothes in the closet, arranged my shoes beneath them, and stashed the towels on a designated shelf in the bedroom cupboard. Pretty soon everything was "ship shape," and as soon as Hamm had the bikes properly assembled, the three of us met under the willow tree.

"I still have to rent a bike so I can get to my overnight digs," June reminded us.

"We can all walk up to the marina office together," I suggested. "Hamm has to pay for our dockage, and the golf cart and bike rental place is right next door, and if they're closed, we can always pay them in the morning."

"That's cool," June replied.

"I'll ride my bike and meet you girls at the office." Hamm hopped on his bike, adjusted his gears, and took off at a leisurely pace.

"I'll need a bike with a basket," June said. "I have to get my clothes and camera gear over to the bed and breakfast, and I'm sure not hauling all that stuff on foot!"

June and I walked my bike up the service road, one on either side, each of us holding on to a handlebar. "What a beautiful day!" I commented, for about the tenth time.

"And I'm actually getting paid to be here," June answered. "Life doesn't get much better."

It was about 4:30, so luckily, there was still about a half hour until the marina office closed. By the time we arrived at the office, Hamm had settled up with the dockmaster and was sitting at a picnic table near the entrance. He was talking to a very handsome dog who apparently wanted to be his new best friend.

"What breed of dog is that?" I had never seen such a big, goofy dog with such a sweet expression.

The dog's owner informed me, "He's a golden doodle, but he's mostly doodle. His name is Joe."

Hamm stood up and gave Joe one last, friendly head rub. "See you later, Joe! Francie, I'll ride back to the boat, and put the dockage ticket in the window. I assume June will want to gather her stuff before we head into town so she can check into her room."

Once again, I wasn't sure if he was being considerate or making sure June was all settled in and wouldn't decide to spend the night with us on the boat. Either way, it was a good plan and we went with it.

June chose a school bus-yellow bicycle with a roomy wicker basket fastened to the front handlebars and a silver carrier rack attached to the rear fender.

"This should do it," she announced, handing her business account credit card to the sales attendant.

We hopped on our respective rides, turned back toward the boat dock, and took off. "Last one back's a rotten egg!" June shouted as she blasted past me.

"Was that a slam on my name?" I countered.

"Don't be so sensitive, Doc!" she shouted over her shoulder, leaving me in the dust.

I realized I wasn't as speedy as I once was. I wasn't exactly huffing and puffing, but I was remembering wistfully how Hamm and I used to ride our twenty-one-speed bikes at home for fun and exercise almost every evening. It was typical back then to log eight to ten miles a day during the week and up to twenty-five miles over the weekend. But that was years ago. We still own those fancy bikes, but now they are mostly collecting dust in the garage. Nowadays, I look forward to tooling around the island on our less deluxe, but more functional marine bikes. It's preferable to paying the tourist's special price of twenty dollars an hour for a golf cart.

Minutes later, June was bouncing off her rented bike, grabbing her essentials, and standing back on the dock grinning, all before I had come to a full and complete stop. The girl hadn't even broken a sweat.

Hamm was also waiting on the dock. "Can we go eat now? I'm hungry." He tucked a cigar in his pocket for later and made sure he had his lighter.

"First stop, Lakeshore Landing." The inn where June would be staying was located west of the marina on Lakeshore Drive. June smiled sweetly in Hamm's direction. "Did you happen to notice that it's only two doors down from Ruby's?"

We rode the short distance and Hamm glanced nervously up the street. "I've been bushwhacked. I should have known better. I give up. You girls go on in and get it over with. I'll wait right here by the rock."

June and I crossed the road and stopped in front of the rambling lakefront home that had been converted into three guest rooms, each with air conditioning and a view of the lake. We hopped off our bikes, forgetting about the usefulness of kickstands. I gave Hamm a big smile and a wave and called out, "Love you!"

After completing the necessary paperwork for check-in and dropping off her bags, June and I hopped back on our bikes, rode across the parking lot and down a short length of sidewalk, and stopped, smiling at the big red door of Ruby's Treasure Chest. Our favorite store would be open for at least another hour.

I hesitated at the door and looked across the street where Hammond was leaning against the wooden railing in front of Inscription Rock.

"Go on inside, June. I'll be in in a minute. I think I'll go make sure Hamm is all right over there."

"Suit yourself. I'm sure I can amuse myself."

I crossed the road and stood next to Hamm, who was reaching in his pocket to retrieve the cigar and lighter he had stashed earlier. He was staring at Inscription Rock, the thirty-two by twenty-one inch limestone rock covered with one of the finest examples of aboriginal art in the Great Lakes region.

"It's amazing to think of how long ago those unusual drawings were created, don't you think?"

"Well, if you ask me," answered my husband, "those petroglyphs look more like dollar signs with wings, laughing shoes, and defeated men than the writings of ancient indigenous people."

"Hey, man, you dropped this." A fit man in running attire stood in front of Hammond, holding his lighter. Hammond snapped out of his preoccupied musings to greet the man who now stood in front of us. He was younger than Hamm, probably closer in age to me and June, but his handsome, serious face had the look of someone who had been through some rough times. His biceps made it clear that it would not be a good idea to challenge him to an arm wrestling match, or any other contest of physical prowess for that matter. His running shoes were not meant to be stylish; they had obviously logged some serious hours of pavement pounding.

"Wow. Thanks. I was killing time while my wife and her friend went across the street behind the evil red door to do lord only knows what to my credit card."

"Hi. I'm Francie, Hamm's wife. I'm not doing any damage yet, but I can accomplish quite a bit in a very short time." I flashed him my sweetest smile.

"I've heard of such things," said the man. He directed his next comment to Hamm. "You're either keeping close tabs on your ladies, or you're hungry and they tricked you with the promise of food."

"The second option. I'm just passing time while they do some shopping, plotting some night maneuvers."

"Excuse me?"

"Oh, don't mind him. Every time we come here, Hamm says the same thing. He's going to carry out clandestine night maneuvers and burn the place down. That way he won't have to go into shock every time the credit card bill arrives."

The stranger held on to Hamm's lighter for a long second before extending his hand to return it. "I'm Jack Morgan. I live here on the island. Maybe I'll see you around. Good luck making it to dinner."

"Thanks," Hamm said. "That was a gift from my wife." I smiled sweetly at the handsome stranger so he was sure to understand what a loving thoughtful wife I was.

"I noticed the inscription. Interesting name. Hammond is it?"

"Yes, you can call me Hamm. Most people do. We come over to the island a lot. This weekend we're docked right over there at Seaway. Stop down for a drink later if you want. I'd buy you one, but I probably won't have any money left when they're through in there. The boat's name is Lucky Enough."

"I just may do that. Nice meeting you both." After shaking hands with Hamm and nodding in my direction, Jack Morgan got right back into his stride, making it look easy.

I took one more admiring look at the runner's physique as he strode off down the road. Remembering why I was here, I turned my attention back to my husband. "I'll be right across the street, sweetie. Enjoy your cigar!"

I didn't give Hamm a chance to object and I didn't look back.

Chapter Six

I pulled open the red door to Ruby's Treasure Chest and immediately saw that June was in the back of the store, camera in hand, pencil in mouth, and notebook tucked under her arm. I stood in the entrance, taking it all in. The walls were covered with unique sculptures, wall hangings, and decorative art, all with a beachy or nautical theme. The right side of the shop held shelf upon shelf of beautiful items for the home, cottage, or boat. My eye was drawn immediately to a glass serving dish in the shape of a fish sparkling with the colors of the sea. I could picture it on the kitchen table of the condo. I was heading toward it to check out the price tag when June's voice interrupted my progress.

"Oh, Ruby, the shop looks wonderful! You've expanded your inventory this year, and that means I'm going to have to expand my own. The hard part of course is that it's going to be impossible to choose between sunglasses, a jacket, or one of those great tote bags. Then there's this entire section back here that I haven't looked into yet. I'm working on an article, you know, about, you know, the new, fun stuff you've added to the shop."

Ruby Burns stood behind the glass front counter watching June through her red rhinestone eyeglasses. Her sturdy body was sheathed in black, but she was in no way somber-looking. Her perfectly manicured, bright red fingernails and toenails matched the shade of her patent leather, low-heeled sandals as well as her name. The wedding ring on her left hand was nothing if not a work of art combining a band of princess-cut diamonds with double bands of blood-red rubies above and below. Everything about her added to her memorable persona.

"For a writer, that June sure has a way with words." Ruby's raspy voice was friendly and welcoming in spite of its deep timbre. She chuckled to herself, tucking a strand of her no-nonsense, gun-metal gray hair behind her ear.

"If you have any questions about anything at all, or if you'd like to try something on, let me know."

"Thanks Ruby. I might have to get some details from you about some of this stuff. For my article, of course."

"Of course, dear. Anything I can do to help."

After I finished eavesdropping on June and Ruby's conversation, I took my time perusing the rest of the aisles and shelves. There were at least five other items I could easily have taken home with me, but I kept going back to the fish plate that caught my eye when I first walked in. I was pretty sure it was coming home with me, but then I remembered the rack of designer scarves that was always located in the back corner of the store. I picked up a gorgeous designer silk scarf in shades of green, aqua, and light blue and held it up against my cheek. How could a simple length of fabric feel so luxurious against my skin? I checked out my reflection in the mirror, but as soon as I saw the price reflected back at me, I put it down. Quickly.

Time for a reality check. I lived in the real world, but it was always fun to fantasize once in a while. Moving on to the last display, I was faced with the one thing that I have always had an absolute true weakness for—a beautiful handbag. I owned a respectable collection, but it seemed there was always room for just one more. I couldn't resist a well-made, soft leather bag in either a traditional or trendy color. I look for lots of interior pockets, a sturdy shoulder strap, and above all, excellent workmanship. No matter where I go, or what I'm doing, I always have a large, beautiful handbag, and it always contains an impressive array of very useful "stuff." I could justify shelling out three figures for a great bag, and I was about to do just that.

I reeled myself back in from temptation, reminding myself that I needed to get my mind off of spending money and back to supporting my friend in her research. Stepping away from the shelf of temptation, I took one last lap around the perimeter of the store. Something caught my eye, and I walked over to the staircase that led up to Ruby's office space to check it out. Beautiful, jewel-toned cut-glass bottles were arranged in a pallet at the foot of the staircase, catching the light from the window and shooting rainbow laser beams up the stairs and onto the ceiling. I came full circle and approached the front counter, directing my attention to the proprietor.

"Ruby, the shop looks great! I think the thing I like best about your place is that everything is always authentic as well as beautiful. You always go out of your way to find local artists, and name brand products that are perfect for your customers. We never have to worry about getting tricked with fakes or counterfeits in here."

A dark cloud skittered across Ruby's expression, but she recovered quickly, broke out her famous smile, and exclaimed in a confident tone, "Oh, I know just what you need!" She beckoned me over to the showcase where she was standing and waved her hand toward the display of sterling silver and crystal beads.

I felt like the proverbial kid in a candy store as I leaned over the sparkling glass case. "You probably put that bead with the wine glasses right up front because you knew I'd be here this weekend!"

"I can box that right up for you, sweetie!" And she did.

Ruby handed me back my husband's credit card along with the small red gift bag. I have never left her shop without one. She was staring out the front window, her gaze coming to rest on the spot where Hamm was nervously shifting from foot to foot. I followed her line of sight, and when I saw what she was looking at, I laughed out loud.

"My poor husband is a little pathetic, don't you think? He teases me constantly about the money I spend here, and how we'd be able to afford a bigger boat if your store would disappear. It's all an act, of course." I took my purchase and glanced out the window just as that gorgeous specimen of male anatomy jogged past the store again, apparently on his way back from wherever it was he came from. He came to a stop in front of Hamm. They had a short conversation, during which time Jack Morgan never stopped moving his feet. He checked his fancy heart rate and pulse-monitoring watch and waved a friendly good-bye as he headed back to complete his evening workout. I might take up jogging too if I had such beautiful scenery to look forward to every day, and I don't necessarily mean the lake and the beach.

Ruby's gaze shifted from the window back toward the corner of the store where June had discovered the section containing the merchandise she needed to "research." There were scented oil-infused candles, romantic CDs, decadent chocolates in red and gold wrappings, even some tastefully sexy lingerie. Nothing lewd or cheesy here. June picked up a silky emerald green camisole. She had an odd, dreamy look on her face.

Handing the expensive nightwear over the counter to be wrapped and ribboned, June commented, "Ruby, these things are fabulous, the best on the island, I'm sure. But now I need something to compare and contrast them with, if you know what I mean. My boss tells me there's a new boutique on the island that might be perfect for my article."

The door chimes jangled and Ruby's husband, Roger, swooped in on a gust of pipe-scented air. "Hello, my friend! Welcome back to the island." He gave me a big hug, nearly spilling the entire tall glass of iced tea he carried with him everywhere. He made a quick save and I discreetly blotted at the dribble of tea on my sleeve, then put some space between his swinging glass and my new white top. "I just talked to your husband across the street. I hear he was making friends with the island's new full-time detective."

"Detective?" June's journalist antennae were vibrating. "Since when?"

"You mean that hottie in the running shorts I just met?" I couldn't help myself. He was definitely a 9.9 on the hunk-o-meter. "Hey, June, if you get into any trouble this weekend, maybe you'll get to meet Detective Dreamy. I'm sure you can come up with some obscure island ordinance that was meant to be challenged."

Roger gave us a conspiratorial look and huddled us closer. Using his top-secret attempt at a whisper, he began. "Yeah. Name's Jack Morgan. He moved here in January. He had to move all his stuff by plane since the ferry wasn't running. This was the first winter in over a hundred years that the lake was frozen solid. Since it's taking so long to thaw, the water is having trouble rebounding to its usual temperature for this time of year." Roger grinned and held his tea-bearing hand in the air. "I certainly wouldn't recommend swimming this afternoon."

"Don't worry, Roger, I don't plan to go in the water until probably the Fourth of July. The thought of that cold water makes me shiver!"

June wanted to hear more about the new resident. "So why was he in such a hurry to move to an island in the middle of a frozen lake?"

"As much trouble as it was, he didn't seem to mind. Looked more like he was in a hurry to get away from something in his old life than to start something new. Rumor has it Morgan used to be a big-city cop in Chicago. His partner and best friend was killed in the line of duty, so he moved to Kelleys Island to get away from the high crime and stress of his job. I think he's dealing with something bigger than your typical grief, myself. I also heard that his partner was his girlfriend, or fiancée, or maybe his wife. I have a hard time keeping all the gossip straight. Maybe you can ask him yourself. He's friendly enough, but keeps his personal life all tucked away. I hear he's very good at what he does and he doesn't always play by the rules. Of course, that's only what I hear. You girls better watch your Ps and Qs while you're here."

All of my attention had been focused on Roger's story, and I hadn't noticed that June had wandered off and was now standing in front of the cash register, exchanging her credit card for another one of Ruby's red bags, which I assumed contained the matching bottom to the pretty camisole she had just purchased.

"I wonder if he likes green." June was evidently thinking out loud as she peeked into the bag containing her second sexy purchase of the day. Who could blame her? She absentmindedly swung the pretty red bag that dangled from her wrist. Her lips were turned up at the corners, and I was pretty sure I could guess what she was thinking about.

The smile on Roger's face lit up the room. His laugh caused his Hawaiian shirt to flap against his ample belly and his glass of tea to wobble dangerously in his beefy grip once again. I backed up a few more inches to avoid another tea splash.

Ruby looked over at June. With a twinkle in her eye, she said to her husband, "Love, maybe you should introduce Detective Morgan to June. Don't you think they'd make a cute couple?"

"Ruby, that's a whale of an idea!" Roger set his sweating glass on the counter so he could take his Ray Bans off the top of his bald head and polish them with the corner of his colorful shirt. He gave June a mischievous wink before putting his mirrored specs back on his face, retrieving his beverage, and heading for the door.

Before he could turn the handle, Ruby stopped his exit with a gentle but firm grip on his arm. "Hold on a minute, Roger. The girls want to make a stop at the new boutique on the other side of the island. What's it called? Oh, yes, Jewel of the Bay. You should probably tell Hamm out there where it is in case these two get turned around and end up lost."

"How do you get lost on an island? Oh. Never mind. All right, I'll go have a chat with the boy."

With his free hand on the doorknob, Roger stopped and swung around. Third time was the charm. Tea sloshed on his knee-high, white athletic socks and soaked his brown leather sandals. Talk about a walking fashion faux pas. But you had to love the guy. I hope I still find Hamm as endearing, with all of his quirks, fifteen years from now.

Framed in the doorway, Roger directed one last comment toward us. "Wait till you gals meet the owner of that place—Sirena Divine! Can you believe that name? Red hair, green eyes, legs up to there... Oh, well, you get the idea. At any rate, she's a flashy one, you betcha!"

As the door shut behind him, we heard Roger's booming voice calling out to Hamm. "It's your lucky day, Hammond! I set you up with another shopping stop!"

Chapter Seven

"Left or right at the intersection?" June hollered over her shoulder to Hamm. She was almost a block ahead of him. I was somewhere in between. "That desk job of yours is doing a number on your legs, counselor! Are your hamstrings getting tight?"

I pretended I didn't hear her. Hamm ignored the jab, but I could tell he was pumping his pedals more vigorously. June rolled her bike to a stop at the intersection and waited for the two of us to catch up. Hamm pulled ahead and rounded the corner to the right. I hung back for a moment, giving him a chance to be the frontrunner long enough to soothe a bruised ego.

When I caught up to him, we rolled along, enjoying the sunshine and warm air for about a quarter of a mile. "What do you think it would be like to live here year-round, Hamm?" I asked.

I admired the houses along the street and imagined myself on a patio overlooking the lake, enjoying the tranquility of island life.

"As much as I love coming here every summer," Hamm replied, "I don't think either of us has it in us to be isolated in the dead of winter, relying on little airplanes for supplies when the lake freezes over." He smiled at me and added, "And what would you do when you ran out of wine?"

"Ouch. So much for that idea."

June hung back. She knew she was getting on Hamm's nerves again, so she amused herself for a while humming the top ten tunes of the eighties.

I was the first to spot the boutique. "Wow! I never knew turquoise sea horses and pink, glass blowfish could look so natural hanging from trees. I have to admit, they give the place a quirky sort of charm."

June stopped singing abruptly and squealed in delight, slamming her bicycle to a halt right in front of an eight-foot tall ceramic mermaid in the yard holding a sign announcing "Jewel of the Bay" in large, multicolored script. This place was right up her alley. Hamm shuddered and braked his bike well away from the surreal seascape.

I was caught off guard and tumbled right into the middle of them. We were doing our best imitation of a three-ring circus bike-stacking act just as a flashy Mercedes E350 Cabriolet convertible flew by shooting gravel and dust all over the three of us. It screamed to a stop in front of the store, inches from Hamm's back tire.

"Hey, asshole! What the hell is wrong with you?"

That was June. I was still gasping for air, and Hamm was glaring at the back of the driver's head. There was something oddly familiar about that rakishly tousled sandy hair and broad shoulders. His starched lavender shirt looked smart against the lunar blue metallic of the car, but was decidedly out-of-place in this laid-back island setting.

When the rude fellow turned around and flashed his professionally straightened and whitened teeth at us, we stopped dead in our tracks. Recognition hit us all and we cried out in unison, "Clifton!"

June was the first to recover. She recognized her ex-husband a split second before Hamm and I did. Funny, how once you realize you know an obnoxious, arrogant person, you become a little more tolerant of his unrefined tendencies. But just a little.

June sprung to the side of the car and stuck her head over the door, mere inches from the driver's face. "What in the name of all things superficial and material are you doing here, Sterling?"

"Well, well, well, it's great to see you too. How are you, Juniper? Francie, Hamm, glad to see the two of you as well!" Sterling took June's arm and began to pat it solicitously.

"Oh for goodness sake. Why are you here? I know you're no fan of fresh air, or for that matter, anything having to do with the outdoors or nature." The arm patting was clearly not working for June, so she shoved his hand off of her bicep and stood about three feet back from the car.

"June, darling, that was harsh. But if you must know, I'm working, actually. Well, mostly."

I was impressed. If this guy was a professional dancer, he couldn't have pulled off a better shuffle.

He continued his explanation. "I met a lovely lady while doing a series on local attractions and vacation destinations. Her name is Sirena. She owns this place."

Talk about a small world. It makes sense though. Both June and Clifton are journalists of sorts. Clifton is the anchorman for the number-three-rated local network, and is on a mission to achieve star status. He never let up trying every trick known and unknown to get his handsome face noticed by the national stations. That he would weasel his way into the good graces of a local shop woman worthy of a centerfold or at least a front page "above the fold" picture, made perfect sense.

Cliff remembered his manners. He exited the vehicle like he was stepping out on a red carpet. He grabbed the linen sports jacket on the front seat, artfully swung it over his shoulder, and swaggered his way over to us. "So, Hamm, aren't you coming inside? You look a little shaky. Sirena's got air conditioning."

"Cliff, my poor husband is shaking because he can't stand the thought of going into the store. He's had this reaction before."

Hamm was allergic to shopping the way Clifton was allergic to trees, grass, pollen, peanuts, and seafood to name a few.

I was tired of standing around. I needed to see what was beyond the beckoning mermaid. I turned back to speak to June, but she had beat me inside.

"You two will have to excuse me. I have to help June with her research."

I gave up on grace and finally threw my bicycle on the top of the heap in the yard while calling out, "Enjoy your visit, boys!"

I left the two men standing by the curb to sort things out in the phantasmic shadow of the giant mermaid and headed into the whimsical shop. June was in the middle of a lively conversation with a most enchanting woman. Even on stage, I had never seen a character like Sirena Divine. I was beginning to wonder if the island suddenly had some magnetic pull, attracting gorgeous new residents.

Sirena was nearly six feet tall. Standing next to June, they were a study in contrasts. Ms. Divine's copper curls cascaded down her back, well past her tiny waistline. Her alabaster skin was luminous. On an island where people compete for the darkest tan, she looked like a pearl in a basket of acorns. I noticed right away that the mermaid on the front lawn bore a striking resemblance to the proprietor. Her long, iridescent skirt flowed around her ankles in waves of aqua, periwinkle, and seafoam. Bright coral toenails peeked out from glittery sandals. I know because I was seriously looking for a fishtail. Sirena was borderline mythical.

June didn't seem particularly dazzled by the lady's ethereal appearance, but it was plain to see she was impressed with her repartee. The two women stood in front of a counter filled with glittering, jewel-toned bottles of essential oils exactly like the bottles I had admired earlier at Ruby's Treasure Chest. Both of them were waving their hands in animated emphasis. This was starting to look like a debate contest. Finally, June got to the point.

"So, how do you know Sterling, Ms. Divine?"

"Oh, he's been in here nearly every day since the first of the month." She seemed quite unaffected by June's straight-up attitude. "He's putting together a piece for his local Sunday morning talk show and seems quite taken with my store."

"I don't think it's the store that has him mesmerized," June informed Sirena. "Clifton has an eye for pretty ladies, especially those who would photograph well. Has he asked you yet to do an on-air companion interview? I'm sure he would love to appear beside you on TV."

Sirena's eyes narrowed. She absentmindedly picked up a small glass vial from the counter display, took the stopper out and inhaled its fragrance. I wanted to ask her what was in it. Maybe I needed some.

Sirena set the pretty bottle down and picked up where she left off with June. "You seem to know a great deal about Mr. Sterling. Have you two met before?"

"You could say that. I was married to him for two years."

As if on cue, Clifton strutted through the front door and took in the scene. He never skipped a beat. Putting his arm protectively around Sirena's waist, he faced June and said, "I see you two are getting acquainted."

You had to give the guy credit. He had an endless capacity for good-natured charm (or bullshit as the case may be). I almost fell under his spell as he smiled his million-dollar smile at me. But I knew better.

"I can't convince Hamm to come inside, Francie. He hasn't changed much, has he?"

I answered him in my head. "Neither have you, Cliff. Neither have you." I smiled politely, took a quick peek out the front window to make sure Hamm was okay, then turned my attention to the pretty seashell serving dishes on the nearest shelf.

Clifton said to June, "Let's all get together later tonight at the Island House. We can catch up over martinis." He directed his attention to me and added, "Bring Hamm. There's no retail, and we can share a nice cigar."

Once more, I smiled, and once more I answered him in my head. "You mean, bring Hamm so you can mooch one of his good cigars." In spite of his powers of attraction, the guy rubbed me the wrong way. Being skilled in the performing arts, I merely smiled politely and nodded.

June didn't seem to hold the same grudge against her former husband. She answered for us all. "We'll be there around eight. Now if you'll excuse us, Francie and I are dying to check out the rest of the store."

Clifton and Sirena took up whispering and giggling like teenagers. They ducked out of sight behind a diaphanous curtain of pearlescent fabric, which I assumed to be a storeroom or an office. I'm sure they had business to attend to. June headed for the back of the store where a sign advertised, "Naughty, Nauti." Cheesy, for sure, but it got my attention.

We spent the next half hour "researching" the merchandise for June's article. We perused the shelves and racks, making copious notes on everything we found. There was an array of provocative clothing from pretty to promiscuous, reading material, massage oils, scented candles in varying sizes, and some mysterious objects I was actually too embarrassed to ask about.

June had left her camera back at the inn, but she used her iPhone to snap pictures of dozens of products and email them to herself. She would have plenty of raw material for her article.

"June, I think we've about overstayed our welcome, and it's almost closing time. We better buy something and head back to town."

I took a last look around and grabbed the most innocuous items I saw: two water rafts each the size of a paperback novel.

The label promised: Just add water for a sassy, sea adventure to remember. Whatever that meant. The twins' birthday was coming up, and I thought they might enjoy some new rafts to float on at the condo pool when they came home for their first summer visit. I figured a person was never too old for a new water toy.

"You must be buying those for your kids, since you can't swim to save your life, and you sure wouldn't want to mess up your hair in a swimming pool!"

"Well, June," I retorted, "at least I don't own a boat I have no clue how to operate!"

I dug around in my royal blue leather bag, which I wore cross-body so I could have two free hands for shopping and bike riding. I located Hamm's platinum Visa card and offered it to Sirena who was back on the sales floor looking flushed.

"Thanks so much for stopping by, ladies. It was so nice to meet you both. I guess I'll see you tonight at the Island House." She smiled sweetly as she rang up my selections then handed my card and purchases over the counter to me.

I tossed my purchases into my handbag where they sunk to the bottom like rocks in a deep well, and headed out the door to rescue Hammond.

"So what do you think of Cliff's new girlfriend?" June asked as I took one last look behind me through the front window.

"June, she winked at me! Why did she wink at me?" June and I glanced back through the window only to see Sirena and Clifton nose to nose, giggling again like teenagers on a first date. "She seems nice enough, but isn't it going to be awkward having dinner with your ex-husband and his new girlfriend?"

June gave a noncommittal shrug. "It doesn't bother me. Cliff and I still get along as well as we ever did. That spark burned out almost as soon as the ink on our marriage certificate dried. I only wish it had happened sooner so we could have avoided all the hassle."

"Yeah, without that spark, as you say, Clifton Sterling becomes a bit less attractive and a lot more like an irresponsible, self-centered child."

"It is what it is. He can be the mermaid's problem now. Besides, if the stars are lined up in my favor, maybe there will be some other gorgeous new islander in need of a dinner companion at the restaurant. They seem to be falling from the trees around here.

Chapter Eight

We needed to get back to the marina so we could get ready for the evening. I felt bad that we never made it back into town for pizza, so I offered to make snacks when we got back. Cheese and crackers would have to do. Hamm and I parted ways with June at the inn and rode the short distance back to the boat where I threw together a nice combination of cheese, crackers and grapes. I was wishing I had that adorable fish plate from Ruby's. I might have to make a return trip.

"Honey, thanks for being so patient today. I know how you feel about shopping. We met some interesting people though, that's for sure. And how crazy was it running into Clifton Sterling of all people?"

"Definitely weird. But that Morgan seems like an alright guy."

"I saw you talking to him again after I went into Ruby's. Did he tell you that he's a detective?"

"He did mention it, and I was glad he found my lighter. There must be a hole in my pocket or something. Can you pass the cheese?"

"Sure thing." I popped a grape in my mouth and handed Hamm the cheese plate.

"He did have kind of an interesting request though. He said to let him know if we heard any strange noises or were awakened by a very loud motor in the middle of the night, particularly around one o'clock. Apparently, there's a small boat that's been coming through the marina late at night. The two people on board use a double-dip hydraulic net to scoop up minnows. I had no idea minnow schools can cover the entire width of the marina. I also had no idea there was a black market for stolen minnows. Apparently, these 'minnow bandits' are selling their stolen fish illegally to fishing charter boat captains. The marina employees have been trying unsuccessfully to identify and capture these guys all last season, and they're back at it already. I told him we'd keep our ears open."

"Maybe we can help solve a mystery! That would be fun!"

"We don't need to set up a spy camp or anything, and you probably shouldn't mention this to June. She'd probably want to turn it into a full-scale, super-sleuth mission. I prefer to relax and leave the detective work to the detective. He probably needs something to occupy his time, anyway. It must be a big adjustment moving from Chicago to Kelleys Island. I don't think I could do it."

"Well, at least the Caddy Shack has great pizza. It can hold its own against Chicago-style any day. And their chicken wings should come with a warning label." My mouth was watering.

"Don't remind me. I never did get mine today."

"Oopsie. We'll put it on our to-do list for tomorrow. I better go get ready for tonight. At least you can order something yummy at the Island House."

"Yeah, this should be interesting."

I left Hamm with the cheese plate and went down to change my clothes for dinner. It was cooling down since the sun was getting lower in the sky, so I chose my black capris, a black-and-white striped tank top and a lightweight white sweater with a hood. Just for fun, I added my red patent-leather flip-flops.

Hamm wouldn't give up his cargo shorts, but he changed into a cobalt blue button-down shirt. June arrived at the boat dock on foot, looking impressive in a white miniskirt and body-hugging navy blue top. She wore a turquoise scarf and turquoise flats that perfectly matched the new color streak in her hair. The turquoise ring on her index finger added a nice finishing touch to her outfit. She bounced on the balls of her feet, practically crackling with energy.

"Let's walk to the Island House," I suggested. Frankly, I had had about all I could take of bike riding for the day.

"Fine with me," June agreed. At least I think that's what she said. She had managed to hop aboard the boat and zero-in on the snack plate. Her mouth was full of crackers.

Hamm and I strolled leisurely hand-in-hand down Division Street toward the heart of downtown and the charming Island House Restaurant and Martini Bar. It was nice not to be in a hurry tonight. June walked a few steps behind, stopping frequently to take casual photos with her iPhone. White picket fences surrounding the property wore mantles of purple clematis blooms and gave the setting both charm and a sense of intimacy. It was such a nice evening, I was glad we had agreed to meet the others at the outdoor bar.

"Hey, June..." I was about to tell her about the minnow bandit mystery, in spite of the fact Hamm didn't think it was a good idea. How could I keep such a bizarre mystery from my best friend? She had dropped back and was stopped on the side of the road. She bent over, affectionately rubbing the ear of a tall, handsome stranger, who happened to be a German shepherd. Accompanying the friendly dog was an intimidating-looking man. I thought special-ops or sniper, but then, I was always running movie scenarios and theater scripts through my mind, and this guy would have been cast as the darkly handsome, unpredictable star of the show. June was acting like she knew the pair. I hoped so because otherwise she was getting pretty desperate to hook up with someone, and that didn't seem like her even though I knew she wasn't looking forward to being the fifth wheel at dinner and watching her ex-husband perform his great-catch act for the benefit of his new love interest.

I later learned that the stranger's name was Michael (no last name) and his dog answers to Gunner. June had uncovered the mystery behind the man and his dog when she met him last summer while spending some leisure time at the lake in between assignments. Michael spends his days coming and going between the islands, Kelleys, Middle Bass, and South Bass, always walking with his dog in silence, always with a steaming cup of coffee in his hand, and always carrying a newspaper tucked under his arm. June couldn't stand the fact that none of the locals knew much of anything about him, so she pursued him for an entire month, pulling out all the stops, using all of her investigative, journalistic, and flirtatious skills until he finally conceded to sit with her for an informal interview.

She never wrote a feature story or even published an editorial about Michael because for all of her in-depth questioning and expert interviewing skills, the only verifiable information she ever got was his name and the fact that he is ex-military and likes his privacy and his dog. She didn't think of the time invested as a waste though because first of all, she wasn't working on a paid assignment, and secondly, she liked him and respected his request to remain private. In the end, June relented, satisfied that at least Gunner had warmed up to her and always stopped for a bit of loving when she encountered him.

After a quick visit, June left the duo and caught up with Hamm and me. I guess he wasn't going to be June's dinner partner after all.

It was a little before eight, and although the patio seating was quickly filling up, we were able to secure a spot on the comfy outdoor sectional couch in front of the unique propane fire top table. From our vantage point, we could see both the outdoor bar and the flower-lined street beyond the fence. I made myself comfortable and started to think about which of several specialty martinis I wanted to order when the sound of a dog bark diverted my attention toward the bar. There was Gunner, accepting attention from the hostess and several of the waiters and waitresses. I got the idea that this was a pretty common occurrence since Gunner was happily lapping water from a big stainless steel dog bowl. Michael, on the other hand, was standing quietly at the bar alone. It almost seemed like he brought a personal space with him that had a Do Not Enter sign clearly displayed on it.

A waitress came out of the restaurant holding a steaming Styrofoam cup which she placed in front of him without saying a word. Michael nodded his head in acknowledgment, never averting his eyes from the newspaper he was reading. The next time I glanced in his direction, he was holding a red pen in his right hand and his coffee in his left. His attention was still focused downward on his reading material. No one joined him or spoke to him. I could see why June was so intrigued with this dark, handsome, mysterious stranger with the loyal, friendly dog. I tried to picture the two of them as a couple. They were polar opposites, yet it wasn't that hard to do.

"What are you daydreaming about over there, Francie?" Hamm raised his hand to get the attention of our waiter. Directing his comment to me, he said, "Since we never did make it to Caddy Shack for pizza, we better order some real food before we start in on drinks. The cheese snacks were good, but it's time for something more substantial. I know your weakness for chocolate martinis, and I also know what happens if you're not careful."

I gave him an appreciative smile. "Well you do have a point. Besides, no one is going to have to twist my arm to make me order something to eat. The hard part will be deciding what to have."

The seat I had chosen was one facing the street with Hamm to my right and June to my left. I wanted to be next to my husband, of course, but I also needed to be within whispering distance of June so we could get in some good-natured gossip about all of the interesting people we saw walking up and down the main street. You never knew when you would see a pirate with a treasure chest full of candy and small toys, and it was good to be ready to embrace the moment. I caught a tootsie roll that rocketed straight at me and looked up just in time to see the handsome pirate tip his three-cornered hat in my direction before continuing on his merry way up the street.

I tossed the treat into my bag for later and retrieved my purse hook so I didn't have to place my handbag on the germy ground. I also grabbed my reading glasses just in case one of the twins happened to text or call me. I was realizing more and more how much I missed them. This was the first summer that both of them were away, and I was starting to understand the day-to-day reality of empty-nest syndrome. Thank goodness for FaceTime. Not that I wasn't enjoying the new freedom that comes with not having to be the responsible parent all the time. It was an adjustment, but it was one I was learning to embrace.

I was finally all settled when I realized I was famished, and my stomach was growling as the tantalizing scent of exotic seasonings, sautéed onions and grilling meat began to fill the evening air.

We got down to the business of studying the menu. Without so much as a glance at the offerings, Hamm ordered the calamari appetizer. He gets it every time. The spicy, sweet Thai-version of this dish is to die for, and it's not offered in many restaurants in this area.

"I think I'll go with the coconut shrimp." It was a hard decision because the lobster mac and cheese was also calling my name. Loud.

There was no hesitation on June's part whatsoever. She chose a lobster sandwich, which consisted of two buns, piled high with lobster and a side of clarified butter. And this was just the first course. I couldn't wait to see what she would order for her entrée.

While we waited for our food to arrive, we talked over all of the interesting things that had happened since we arrived. "Bingo!" June shouted, interrupting Hamm's retelling of his chat with the detective. "Bingo, Bingo, Bingo!"

I looked in the direction of June's open-mouthed stare. "Bingo" was our code word for something demanding immediate attention. Standing at the bar, in the same spot Michael had occupied, was an older man dressed entirely in neon orange spandex. On his head, covering his grey dreadlocks, was a pink-and-blue striped stocking hat. And if that wasn't enough, he was wearing high heels and sipping a drink topped off with a miniature umbrella. I almost choked.

"Now there's something you don't see every day," I said, once I regained my composure. "People are pretty amazing. You've got to love a free spirit!"

Our food arrived and we lost interest in the colorful man at the bar, directing our attention to the plates in front of us. My shrimp was prepared with the perfect combination of sweetness and crunch, and Hamm was evidently pleased with his choice as always.

June looked up from her decadent selection and smiled. "Don't underestimate the magical powers of this butter!" I think I gained three pounds just watching her eat it.

We were finishing up our yummy hors d'oeuvres when Clifton and Sirena arrived. Heads turned. People stared at the beautiful couple. I couldn't help but think of Jay Gatsby and Daisy Buchanan. Except for the tattoo. Sirena's low-cut, clingy tank top revealed more than her fabulous figure. An intricately executed scorpion decorated her chest above her heart. Its tail curled provocatively up and to the right. I had no idea where its head was. Sirena seemed oblivious to the attention; Clifton, on the other hand, was basking in it. I seriously thought he might take a bow, or worse yet, make a speech. He did neither. He plopped into the seat across from me, reached across the table, and absent-mindedly popped the last of my shrimp into his mouth. June stopped mid-greeting and stared agape at Clifton.

"Francie, quick! Grab the EpiPen in your purse!"

"What's the matter?" Sirena was frantically looking from Clifton to June to me. I was rummaging in the bottom of my voluminous handbag, where sure enough, I located the EpiPen I had stashed there months ago in case one of my kids had an allergic reaction to something sometime. How June knew it was in there was beyond me. She grabbed it from my hand and reached across the table to stab the gasping man across from me.

So much for Jay Gatsby. Clifton was furiously scratching the ugly red hives that had blossomed on his cheeks and neck. His lips were swollen and his eyes had all but disappeared. At least he was breathing.

"Should we call the EMS?" Sirena seemed genuinely concerned about her companion's welfare.

"He'll be fine." June explained to Sirena that her ex-husband was plagued with a plethora of allergies, "literally from soup to nuts." The island's makeshift medical clinic would likely have provided him with the exact same treatment.

"I had no idea Cliff's allergies were that bad," Sirena remarked. "Frankly, he never mentioned the fact he had them."

Go figure, I thought.

"I knew allergies could be severe, and sometimes even fatal, but I've never seen anything come on so quickly. Maybe I should invest in one of those EpiPens myself."

"Probably not a bad idea," June answered. "Not only does Clifton's vanity keep him from advertising his flaws, but he also has some issues with impulse control. Just saying."

Chapter Nine

When Clifton could speak again, he humbly thanked both June and me for saving him from death, if not embarrassment. I could see it was an effort for him to speak through his slightly less bulbous lips, and after that, he sat quietly like a chastised schoolboy for a long time while we chatted with Sirena. I begrudgingly admitted to myself that I liked her.

Hamm asked her about the travails of starting up a new business on an island. "The logistics alone of getting your merchandise over from the mainland must have been a daunting task, especially doing it all on your own."

Sirena leaned in close to Hamm and replied, "Everyone on the island has been so welcoming and helpful. I got a lot of good advice from a local lady, Ruby Burns. She and her husband, Roger, gave me contact numbers for merchants and vendors on all of the islands as well as on the mainland. They were so nice especially considering I'm in direct competition with her business. They seemed to know everything about everyone. The only thing Ruby had a hard time with was remembering my name. She has a beautiful gift shop here. Do you know her?"

The conversation was taking a dangerous turn toward the topic of shopping. Hamm needed a diversionary tactic. Quickly he asked, "How about drinks? This round is on me. I think Cliff could use a nice glass of bourbon about now. I know what Francie wants. June, how about you?"

I looked suspiciously at my husband. Was he being nice to June? I wondered if he was trying to impress Sirena. Oh, well. I was having a good time and wasn't about to spoil the mood. Getting into the spirit, I asked Sirena, "Have you tried the chocolate martini? It's called the Diva with good reason.I don't know how they do it, but you won't find a better one anywhere. Ever."

Sirena answered me quickly. "I hear they're fabulous, but I'm a one cocktail kind of girl. Vodka martini, dry, with a lemon."

"That sounds refreshing and it's hard to mess up a good martini, but you should try the chocolate martini at least once. You won't be sorry."

"I'll keep that in mind," Sirena answered politely.

"I'll have a Jack Daniels over ice." The drink selection was familiar, but the voice ordering it was not. We all turned to the newcomer who had just placed his order. He wasn't butting in as I assumed. The waiter just happened to be standing right behind Hammond.

"Hey, it's you!" Hammond and the man said simultaneously. Then they both laughed. I recognized him as the runner, or detective as the case may be, I met talking to my husband outside Ruby's Treasure Chest earlier in the evening, and he was every bit as handsome as the first time I saw him.

"I see you survived your shopping expedition."

"I did. But we never did make it over to Caddy Shack for pizza."

"Well, if you're hungry, this place makes the best hamburgers on the planet. And trust me, I know my burgers."

"Thanks, Jack. I'll survive. I've given up many meals over the years because of shopping diversions. Jack Morgan, you remember my wife, Francesca. And this is June, her friend. And this..."

Jack interrupted. "Oh, I know these two. Sirena is a neighbor, and I met Mr. Sterling the first day he arrived on the island. We had a chat about his treating our rural roads like the Indy 500." Clifton shrugged in reply. He was looking much better, but didn't seem to want to take the risk of talking out loud.

Hamm stood and shook Jack's hand. "Please join us, Jack. You can't be all bad since you ordered the same drink I was about to."

So there we were. A nice even six. Our drinks arrived and we settled into friendly conversation. June and Super-Hunk, I mean Jack, quickly discovered they had absolutely nothing in common—nothing, that is, except some invisible connection linking their gazes.

Hamm raised his glass and toasted. "Here's to a relaxing, long weekend with no agenda and no worries."

"Here, here!" Clifton, Sirena and I agreed all at once. June and Jack came in a half beat later.

Winter survival stories gave way to summer plans for cruise destinations, picnics, parties, and for some of us, new shopping adventures. Sirena and June got into an animated conversation, swapping stories about entrepreneurship, freelancing, and the trials and joys of being self-employed single women. June practically had to sit on her hands because I could tell she wanted to write everything down. She was getting some great information on the new store owner on the island that she could easily incorporate into her article. Luckily her memory was even better than her shorthand.

"Cliff, are you up for an evening smoke?" Hamm slipped a sleek leather case from his pocket and removed two of his favorite cigars, offering one to Clifton.

"Man, thanks. I would love to but I'm not sure I could hold a cigar between these water balloon lips of mine, and my lungs are feeling a little tight after that stupid shrimp fiasco. I'll have to take a rain check."

"It sucks to be you, Sterling." I did not say that out loud, did I? I needed to be careful. If I had another martini, I was sure to get myself in trouble. I was surprised Cliff made that self-deprecating remark. Maybe Sirena was having a positive effect on him. Miracles do happen.

"How about you then, Jack? A good cigar is always better with company."

"I couldn't agree more, but one a day's my limit, and after talking to you earlier, I went home and enjoyed one of my own on my deck. Perfect way to finish off a five mile run, right?"

"Well, as Harry Callahan always said, 'A man's got to know his limitations.'"

"*Dirty Harry*, right? Now that was a classic movie. I wish there were programs on now that were intelligent and entertaining instead of all those 'reality' shows that are as far from real as you can get."

"I can appreciate that, Jack. You're a man after my own heart. Then if you all don't mind, I think I'll take a walk down toward the boats and smoke this by myself. There's something to be said for peace and quiet. I could use some after all the shopping excitement I had to endure today."

"There is that." I did a double-take when Jack replied with one of Hamm's famous sayings. I wasn't sure what to think about that.

Hamm gave my hand a squeeze and pressed a wad of bills into my fist. "Have another drink on me." I smiled up at my husband and gave him a return hand squeeze. I was fine with him leaving. We had been married for twenty-two years. That doesn't happen without some give and take.

Clifton's wistful gaze in the direction of the marina was proof of where he would rather be. Who was he to complain? He was with the most beautiful woman on the island. And she didn't even run screaming when he morphed into a shrimp-induced, misshapen monster.

Sirena rose and excused herself from the table. "I'll be right back, Clifton. Nature calls. I'll have another of the same if the waiter comes by while I'm gone."

As she headed toward the door, I saw her take her cell phone from a deep pocket in her skirt and quickly scroll through her text messages. For a split second, her face was reflected in the glass door leading to the inside of the restaurant where the restrooms were located. I couldn't know what she saw, but her expression reminded me of a brewing thunderstorm.

While Sirena was still in the restroom, our second round of drinks arrived. "Those look wonderful!" I paid the waiter and added a generous tip with the money Hamm had slipped me before he headed back toward the lure of his cigar.

"I know that guy," Morgan said, directing his gaze to the small stage on the patio. "I'm surprised he doesn't perform in much bigger venues. He's got talent."

We admired the guitarist's talent strumming island tunes until he stopped singing and stood up to make an announcement.

June snuck in an observation before the entertainer spoke. "It seems like there are several people around here with big city talents who would rather concentrate on living a simpler life than chasing fame and fortune."

Jack gave her an appraising look, but before he could come back with a response, the announcement began.

"The final entry into the drawing for couples to win a chance to be named Island King and Queen in the upcoming Memorial Day parade will be ending in five minutes. Both entrants must be present at the bar to register, so grab your partner and get on over!"

Cliff craned his neck in the direction Sirena had gone and was practically vibrating with urgency. I could tell that his need for fame and validation was getting the best of him. He wanted in that contest in the worst way. Sirena hadn't yet returned when the final call was being made to enter. Before I knew what hit me, Cliff grabbed my arm, pulled me to my feet, and started dragging me between tables of startled diners toward the bar.

"What in the name of King Kong are you doing, Sterling? Let go of me! We're going to kill ourselves dodging tables like this."

"You have to sign up with me in Sirena's place for Island King and Queen Francie. Come on, hurry!"

"Oh you are going to owe me big time for this, Clifton."

We made it to the registration table by the bar at the last second. We each filled out an entry form, with me standing in for Sirena. I completed Sirena's entry with the information Cliff whispered to me line by line. Once the ballots were secured and sealed in the official envelope, I began winding my way back to our table. I didn't wait for Clifton to catch up, but I did decide he would be buying my next drink.

When I got back to our table, I noticed June had moved over so she was sitting right beside Jack Morgan. They were both humming along off-key to Faith Hill's "Sunshine and Summertime" that was playing through the speakers while the emcee was finishing up his contest preparations. I settled back into my chair and returned to my drink. Sirena's chair was still vacant.

"Maybe you should go check on Sirena. Do you think she's okay?" Clifton was tapping his thumbs and index fingers nervously on the table. I was sipping my martini, and June and Morgan were still oblivious to their surroundings as well as their lack of musical talent.

"Do you think she ditched me?" I had never heard Clifton express the smallest amount of self-doubt, so this got my attention. Before I could decide whether to be nice or snarky, Sirena strolled back toward the table.

"Sorry I took so long. There was a line. Oh, drinks! Don't mind if I do."

She reached for the vodka martini on the table but stopped short of picking it up. Pulling her eyebrows together, she whispered,"Why would they put a lemon in a perfectly good drink?" I was the only one close enough to hear her comment, and I wasn't positive that was what she said. "On second thought, I think I'll pass on the drink. Cliff, darling, maybe we should call it a night. You had quite an eventful evening, and I've got a long day ahead of me tomorrow."

"It would be a shame to leave fresh drinks on the table. Let's stay a few more minutes. I can drive you back to your boutique or your house in under five minutes."

Leave it to Clifton. One minute he was all worried about his new girlfriend's true feelings toward him and the next he's taking the risk of making her mad over a drink, more specifically, a free drink.

Sirena sat back down, gave Cliff a forced smile, and picked up her martini glass. She swirled the drink in the glass, raised it to her lips, hesitated, and set it down without taking a sip. Her mind was most definitely somewhere else.

Remembering the look on her face when she checked her phone on her way to the restroom, I debated whether to ask her if everything was all right or to keep my mouth shut and mind my own business. Before I could make up my mind, the tooth-jangling wail of sirens sliced through the peaceful air—many sirens: fire, police, and ambulance, all streaking past us in the direction of the marina.

Cocktail conversation morphed into excited, curious, and fearful speculation all around us. Cell phones lit up like lighters at a rock concert. Everyone was trying to be the first to discover what the event was that was causing this spectacular disruption.

Jack's brow furrowed. He squinted down at the screen of his smartphone.

"I've got to go. Something is going on, and the police chief wants me to head over to the station. I guess they can use all the help they can get. If you all will excuse me."

We never got a chance to pump him for information. He was up and on the sidewalk before June could form words. Amazing, I know.

Jack hesitated a second on the street before calling over the fence, "Hey, Cliff! I need to borrow your car."

Clifton didn't hesitate. He was not about to toss his keys to a virtual stranger who moments ago was nose-to-nose with his wife, okay, ex-wife. He sprinted to the curb and leapt into the driver's seat of his sports car. "Where to, Detective? Clifton Sterling at your service!"

Jack didn't have time to argue. He got in the passenger's seat, and the tires squealed as they sped off.

June and I stared at one another, baffled at the sudden turn of events. Sirena's gaze was locked on some invisible point down the street. Other patrons were shuffling out of their seats to get a better look at who-knows-what.

"What should we do now?" I didn't have a plan.

June looked at Sirena and me then down at the three perfectly executed martinis standing at attention on the table.

"Well, I have to agree with Cliff for once on this one. It would be a shame to let these drinks go to waste. We can't do anything to help since we don't have a clue what's going on."

I thought about what she said. "That sounds reasonable. We can head back to the boat once all the commotion dies down. Maybe Hamm saw something and can fill us in when we get back."

Sirena's nose wrinkled as she pushed herself away from the table. "Suit yourself, ladies. I think I need to go."

I couldn't identify the strange look on her face or the words she mumbled to herself as she left.

"What do you think that was all about? She seemed awfully distracted.

Chapter Ten

June sipped her drink, staring out across the road. "Well, what do you expect? She's left sitting here with her new squeeze's former partner. That had to be awkward. Plus, she doesn't know us, and she's probably worried about her store. Everyone seems to be heading in that direction. It is a shame about her cocktail though."

I watched Sirena stride resolutely away from us. "Hey, check it out, June. She isn't a goddess after all. She has toilet paper stuck to the seat of her skirt."

"Hmmm. Looks more like a dryer sheet to me. At least it proves she's human like the rest of us."

The excitement was winding down almost as quickly as it had begun. We sipped our drinks and speculated on all the possible causes for the mad rush.

"Maybe we should be more concerned. Everyone was headed in the direction of the marina. I hope our boat is okay. Maybe there was a big bust and they captured those minnow bandits Hamm told me about. Maybe they had guns or there was a fight."

"What the heck are you talking about? What's a minnow bandit?"

"Oh, sorry. I never got the chance to tell you. It's a pretty strange story. Morgan asked us to be on the lookout for..."

June interrupted. "Jack is very interesting, don't you think? Cute too. I'm sure whatever the commotion was, he has it handled. Do you think he'll be back?"

"Don't you want to hear about the minnow bandits? I thought you wanted to hear about the minnow bandits."

"I do Francie, but I'm thinking we've been here long enough. Our party's over. The authorities are out doing their thing. We should be sensible and head back to the marina for the night."

"You're right," I sighed. "I'm probably overreacting."

June and I looked at Sirena's abandoned drink, thought better about what was running through both our minds, and pushed back from the table.

We covered the half mile distance back to the marina, chatting and speculating on what all the commotion was about, and came to the conclusion that we might as well wait for morning when everything would be sorted out.

When I got to our boat, the first thing I noticed was there were no lights on inside the boat. The area in front of it was shrouded in complete darkness. "Hammond, what are you doing in the dark? Hamm? Honey?"

Within seconds of getting onboard and flipping on a light, it was obvious Hammond was not in the cabin. I hurried back out to the cockpit and after my eyes adjusted to the dark, I scanned the dock, thinking maybe he was enjoying the view while finishing his cigar. He wasn't on the dock, so I looked out toward the lake.

Then I saw him. He was heading toward the boat from the direction of the grassy area that led to the small strip of beach and the lake beyond.

I stepped off the boat and onto the dock, planning to meet him halfway. When he got close enough to hear me, I called out to him.

"There you are. I was getting worried. Did you find out...?"

I stopped mid-sentence when I got close enough to see Hamm's appearance. He was carrying his shoes, his cargo shorts were torn, and there was a dark stain on the front of his new shirt.

"What the... Where the... Why do you smell like a campfire?"

I was at a loss. In all our years together, I had never seen Hammond so disheveled. I had, however, seen that look on his face before. "Get the front lines ready. We're leaving. Now!"

"Are you sure you want to do that, Hamm? I've had a few drinks and don't think I'm steady on my feet enough to be manning lines and fenders in the dark. It's getting late, hon. why don't you get some sleep and we can talk about this in the morning?"

"Whatever." Hamm didn't say anything else, but I was relieved when he walked past me and headed into the boat. He closed the cabin door behind him.

I had no way of knowing the source of Hamm's foul mood or the cause of his uncharacteristic appearance, but I did know that now was not the time to ask him about it. I also knew that any attempt to engage my husband in civil conversation would probably result in tears on my part, so I left him alone and joined June, who was sitting at the picnic table on the dock in front of the boat.

"So what was that all about? Did I do something to make him mad? I thought I was behaving. I'm guessing this is all my fault as usual."

"It is so not your fault." I was confident of this at least. Something much bigger was eating Hamm, and by the end of the weekend, we would both know what it was. I was wide-awake now. Sleep didn't seem to be in my immediate future.

"It's such a beautiful night. Why don't we sit out here for a while? I should probably give Hamm some space right now. He doesn't seem to want company."

"That's an understatement. Are you sure he won't get mad if we hang out?"

"June, he's not mad at you, or at me for that matter. I'm sure in the morning he'll tell me all about whatever happened that's got him so upset."

"Okay then, I wouldn't mind some girl time."

I waited about five minutes before I went aboard the boat to use the bathroom and put my sunglasses away. Hamm was snoring softly on the couch, still wearing his dirty, torn clothing and smelling like he had been roasting marshmallows at a campfire. He didn't stir, and I was back on the dock in no time.

The moon was high in the sky, reflecting in the water and creating an otherworldly effect on our surroundings. We sat with our own thoughts for a few minutes, but since girlfriends are not capable of extended periods of silence unless they are fighting, June leaned over and whispered, "What do you think about all of the commotion earlier? I wonder where Clifton and the detective ended up. Did you think Sirena was acting kind of odd? And you've got to be wondering what on earth happened to Hamm. I feel like we stepped into an episode of the Twilight Zone."

We had been on the island less than a full day, but it seemed like ages since the cruise across the lake. We talked for over an hour, replaying the events of the day until we had exhausted every scenario and possible outcome.

No sooner had I stood to stretch my legs when the sound of a powerful outboard motor broke the peaceful atmosphere. "Quick, June, get down!"

"What are you flipping out about, Francie? It's just a boat."

I never did fill June in on the details of the strange request Hammond had received from Detective Morgan while we were inside Ruby's Treasure Chest. How had I forgotten?

"Duck down and be quiet! See if you can see who's driving the boat or any identifying numbers or information on the hull."

"What's this all about, Francie? I feel like Harriet the Spy."

I gave her the Reader's Digest version of the tale of the minnow bandits, and as soon as I stopped talking, I could see that she was all in.

"Let's nail these greedy thieves. I'd love to get a first-hand interview and go home with two awesome articles. I might be able to take the rest of the summer off at this rate."

We crouched behind the picnic table, straining our eyes to make out any clues. The boat passed slowly right in front of us. Two men who couldn't have been more than twenty were working their scam right before our eyes. A tall, skinny kid worked the hydraulic nets while his beefy partner scooped hundreds of tiny, silver, squirming fish into rows of buckets. They had this fish-napping thing down to a science. We had to concentrate on all the details, trying to commit everything to memory since neither of us had our cameras or phones nearby. I didn't even have a pencil or paper since my handbag was back in the boat. It never fails. As soon as I set it down out of reach, I need something. For lack of a better plan, I focused on memorizing the twelve-digit hull identification number displayed on the right side of the transom. Apparently, the brilliant criminals hadn't thought to conceal the numbers that could quickly identify all the information about the boat and its owner. June took mental notes on the physical features and clothing of the two brazen entrepreneurs.

The boat finished its mission and left the marina, heading east. As soon as it was out of sight, I unfolded my body from its awkward position under the picnic table and went in search of pen and paper. when I stepped on board.

When I entered the cabin, Hammond was sitting up rubbing the stubble on his cheeks "What was all that racket about? I was sound asleep. Hey, what time is it? Maybe it was those guys the detective told me about."

"Oh, honey it was them. I need to write this down before I forget. Let's see: OH55 5SPF 1029. I can't wait to bust these goons!"

"Well, it'll have to wait at least until morning. What are you doing up so late anyway?"

"June and I were just talking about everything that happened today. Did you ever find out what all the sirens were about?"

"No. I had my own problems. I'm going to bed."

I wanted to ask about his clothes and his mood, but I decided I would let it go until morning. Technically, it was morning, but I needed to get some sleep before the sun came up and shed light on the day's baffling events.

I went back outside to say goodnight to June and found her pacing back and forth on the dock. "Hey, Francie, I'm all wound up. Can I borrow your bike and ride back to the bed and breakfast? That should give me time to unwind before trying to get in a few hours sleep. I'll bring it back in the morning. If Hamm still wants to go back to Beacon Pointe, I'd like to come along if he doesn't mind."

"I don't know, June. It's awfully late."

"Don't be silly. There are street lamps the whole way back, and there won't be any traffic, that's for sure!"

I was reluctant to give in, but I knew she'd wear me down until she got her way. "Okay, fine. At least promise to text me when you get back safely. I'll wait up."

She was balanced on the seat and ready to take off. As she rode away, she called back to me, "I'll text you in a few minutes. Bye!"

As promised, five minutes later, I received the short message "home safe c u in am."

Relieved that all was well, I changed into my pajamas, fell into bed, and was out in seconds.

Chapter Eleven

Shortly after sunrise, much earlier than I wanted to be up and around, I awoke to the glorious smell of Starbucks Breakfast Blend. I lay under my cozy down comforter torn between staying tucked into my comfy berth or giving in to the lure of caffeine. I couldn't ignore the aroma any longer, so I tossed my pillow aside and followed my nose to the coffee. I poured a generous mug and shuffled out to the cockpit where I found Hammond staring out at the placid water, cradling his own steaming cup. The morning was peaceful, and as I sipped my coffee, I thought about what had caused my husband's mood to change from lighthearted to sour last night.

We had paid for dockage for the three-day holiday weekend, and I was certain that if we left now, our dock would be reassigned, and we wouldn't be able to return if we wanted to. I sat down beside my husband and drew my legs up onto the seat so I could scoot them under Hamm's legs. Judging by the fact he allowed me to touch him with my feet, which he usually hates, I figured it was okay to proceed with my questions.

"So, honey, are you ready to talk about last night?"

I couldn't read the expression in his eyes. Frustration? Guilt? Helplessness? He rubbed my knee and continued to look out to the water. Much as I wanted to question him, I pressed my lips together and waited.

"First of all, when I went to light my cigar, my lighter was gone again. I was upset—I mean twice in one day. But I didn't feel like walking all the way back into town to look for it. I found a pack of matches from the Island House in my shirt pocket, and I don't remember putting them there. I wasn't drunk, that's for sure, so all this weird stuff started getting to me."

Again I swallowed the words welling up in my throat. He took a sip and continued.

"While I was down near the lake, smoking my cigar, I heard the sirens. I guess I was so distracted looking at the emergency vehicles whizzing by that I didn't notice a snuffed-out campfire near the edge of the water. I tripped right over it and ruined my shorts, scuffed up my new shoes, and lost my cigar. I'm sorry I got so upset. I guess the combination of June and Cliff and shopping just had me on edge. Then there's the fact I keep losing things. You know it takes me awhile to learn how to relax at the beginning of the summer and get used to our weekend friends. I was mad at myself more than anyone."

The corner of his lip twitched. "And you know I'm sorry about June's assignment. She's good at her job, and she seemed to be enjoying herself. I also noticed there were some interesting dynamics starting up between June and Jack." There was that lip twitch again.

"I'm sure June got enough material to work with. If not, she knows her way back to Kelleys if need be. She comes here a lot on her own, you know. There's also the Internet, which she probably could have used in the first place. But a trip to the island is so much more intriguing. I noticed some exchanging of phone numbers happening over dinner, too. This might get interesting. How about a refill on that coffee?"

He held his cup out to me and I brought our mugs down to the galley for refills. We spent the next half hour or so lingering over our brews and speculating about the cause of the sirens and commotion the night before. We accomplished nothing. No, that's not true. The tension between us was gone and the man beside me was no longer a stranger.

By eight, June was back at the dock as promised. My bike was parked right beside Hamm's; she had returned her rental bike, and now she was standing by, awaiting orders from the captain. I realized that in spite of our reconnection over coffee, Hamm was still determined to return to the mainland.

I tried to hide my disappointment as we performed all the duties required in preparation for getting underway. June took charge of the water hose and electric cord while I made my way to the bow of the boat, unhitched the dock line from the cleat, untied the spring line, and waited for my cue to push off.

Once Hamm had maneuvered the boat out of the marina and set his course, June and I relaxed and curled up on either side of the wraparound seat.

"This isn't what I had planned for the holiday weekend by any stretch of the imagination. You didn't have to come back with us, but thanks. You had such a nice room, and you seemed to have something starting up with the handsome detective."

"Nonsense! My boss paid for my room, and I'll probably take the ferry back tomorrow for the parade. I'm dying to find out who will be crowned the new King and Queen. Maybe it will be Clifton and you!" She laughed, and before I could reach over and smack her, she added, "Sorry, I meant Sirena."

"Ha, ha. Very funny."

"Jack Morgan isn't going anywhere either, and I know where he lives. Well, not the exact location, but hey, we're talking Kelleys Island not Chicago or New York. Besides, it'll be nice to spend one night on the houseboat and get caught up with everyone on the dock. Meanwhile, we might as well decide what we are going to wear tonight."

"I guess you're right. I wasn't planning on it, but since we'll be back at Beacon Pointe anyway, we can go to the yacht club Memorial Day party tonight. We'll have to figure out what food we're going to bring too."

So we spent the rest of the short trip back to the marina discussing and deciding on the important matters of what to wear and what to eat.

"See you tonight. Thanks for everything!" June hopped off the boat and high-tailed it toward her houseboat as soon as we pulled into our dock slip and secured the lines.

Some of our friends were socializing on the dock, drinking coffee, taking advantage of the nice weather, and getting caught up with all the latest news. June got right in the middle of a debate over whether the monthly yacht club parties should be potlucks or catered. I wasn't in the mood to get into that conversation.

Hamm connected the power and water before heading down below to take a much-needed shower. I didn't mention it to him, but I was thankful he would finally be getting the lingering smell of smoke out of his hair. I felt like lying low for a bit and mulling over some of the strange things that had happened. I turned on the cabin TV and tuned in to the local news channel for the sake of background noise while I made a list of ingredients I would need to put together a nice Mediterranean pasta salad for tonight. I had everything except cherry tomatoes back at the condo, and I could get those at the Beacon Pointe Market.

Just then I remembered what was niggling at the back of my mind. I put on my glasses so I could read the series of letters and numbers I had jotted down the night before. I had a more pressing matter than buying tomatoes to tend to.

"Hello, this is Francesca Egge. I need to speak to Detective Morgan, please." While I was on hold, I went over the details June and I had uncovered about the minnow bandits last night.

"Morgan here. How can I help you?"

"Hello, Detective. I have some information you may find useful..."

After my conversation with the detective, I felt much better, but I still had so many questions I wanted to ask Hamm.

As if on cue, he came out of the bathroom, smelling like Irish Spring with a hint of my herbal shampoo. A mischievous smile spread across my face as I reached for the towel around his waist. "Hey, good looking! I have an idea of what to have for breakfast." Suddenly, I forgot everything I was going to ask him.

After I showered and dressed in white shorts and a pink T-shirt, I towel-dried my hair and headed for the coffee pot to brew a second pot so we could have a do-over of our early morning routine. Hamm was finally feeling relaxed and had gone out to the cockpit to wait for me. Things were returning to normal.

While I stood at the counter, waiting for the world's slowest coffee pot to finish its job, I straightened up the cabin, made the bed, wiped down the counters, and washed the glasses from last night. I started feeling kind of bad again that June had paid for a room on the island and wasn't using it until I remembered her boss had footed the bill. Still, it would have been nice for her to spend the night in a clean, cozy bed and breakfast and wake up ready to enjoy the Memorial Day festivities on the island. For that matter, it would have been nice for Hamm and I to be there as well. Oh well, we were making the best of the situation. The coffee wasn't quite ready, so I attempted to tame my unruly hair and apply a dash of color to my face.

As I was swiping on the last bit of mascara, I heard the first notes of "Girls Just Want to Have Fun" chirping on my cell phone. I managed to grab the phone and silence the ring before the chorus finished. It was the ringtone I had assigned to June, and I was fairly certain that it would be an unwelcome interruption to Hamm's emerging relaxed state of mind.

"Hang on a second, June. I'll be right back."

I poured Hamm a cup of coffee, brought it out to him and informed him, "I'll be right back, dear."

Back in the cabin, I grabbed my phone.

"Hey, what's up?"

I could barely make out what she was frantically whispering over the line. It sounded like she was in a wind tunnel.

"What's going on? Speak up. I can barely hear you."

"Listen, Francie. Something weird is going on. I took a cab into town this morning to hit the farmer's market for the ingredients to make my strawberry rhubarb dessert for the party tonight. I know Hamm likes it, and I thought it might make him feel better. As I was getting ready to leave, I swear I saw Sirena and some guy behind the vendor's barn practically duking it out. He grabbed her arm, and she turned around and slapped him. You've got to come out here and tell me I'm not imagining things."

My hand went to my forehead and I closed my eyes, trying to fight the urge to scream.

"I'm in the middle of my morning cup of coffee with my husband, June. You might have misunderstood the situation. Besides, Hamm will be thoroughly irritated if I take off right now. He's finally starting to relax."

"I'm serious, Francie. I wouldn't have bothered you if I didn't think we needed to do something to help. I wouldn't feel right approaching her by myself though, being Cliff's ex and all. She might think I was spying on her or something."

"Well you kind of are, June. What exactly do you propose we do?"

"I'm going to sit here at the picnic table by the entrance and keep an eye on them until you get here. I'll have a plan by then."

"I don't suppose I can talk you into forgetting this and coming back to the marina. I can whip up some pancakes and help you prepare your dessert for tonight. Or we could go to the condo and have breakfast on the deck."

"I knew I could count on you, Francie. I'll see you in ten."

It was the exact response I had feared. I guess I had to break the news about my early-morning trip to my husband. She lures me in every time.

Chapter Twelve

I was resigned to using our gas-powered golf cart to make the mile-and-a-half trip down to the open-air market near the heart of town. Hamm decided after some half-hearted grumbling that he would go into Port Clinton to the marine store while I was gone. He had been hinting since last fall that he could use some new dock lines and was content enough to go purchase some boat accessories while I was gone. I found it amusing that Hamm could spend hours at West Marine comparing prices, asking questions, and ultimately standing at a cash register with his credit card extended without making the connection that what he was doing could only be defined as shopping.

I felt a twinge of guilt about telling him June had forgotten her wallet when she went to the market and that she asked me to bring it to her, but when I mentioned that she was going to make his favorite dessert, he kissed me on the cheek and told me to have fun and take my time.

Hamm doesn't usually approve of June-fueled mystery adventures because generally they end us up in some sort of hot water. I don't ever lie to my husband per se, but sometimes I find it expeditious to give a little twist of fantasy to events that might cause him to suffer undue stress. My real job has me constantly running through script edits, looking for exactly the right spin to put on a story. So now, as I chugged along the winding bayside road in my golf cart, I ran through every possible explanation for the encounter June said she had witnessed between Sirena and some mystery man. First of all, what would Sirena be doing off the island so early this morning? Didn't she have a business to attend to? Was it even her, or had June's imagination gotten the best of her? And what about all the commotion last night? She seemed awfully determined to get away from us. Maybe this trip wouldn't be a waste of time. Maybe I'd get some answers.

It was a beautiful morning. Lakeside daisies were blooming in the fields along the side of the road, popping up among nearly barren, limestone bedrock. I remembered when I first saw the frilly, yellow flowers and learned that they are Ohio's rarest, native plant species. This plant only grows in four areas, its largest population being right here on the Marblehead peninsula. Even though cars were passing me and honking at my slow progress, I tried to concentrate on the joy of driving through this little-known garden of endangered species.

I amused myself by holding my left hand out and watching my color-changing nail polish turn from pearl white to flamingo pink in the sunlight and almost missed my turn onto the dirt drive that led to the market. I kicked up some dust, and nearly missed running smack into Michael and Gunner walking away from the market entrance.

"Sorry, guys!" I waved and pulled into the entrance to find June. It wasn't difficult. She was seated at a picnic table, peeking over the top of a newspaper like a spy in a B-movie.

"What in the actual heck took you so long, Francie? I've been sitting here for hours!"

"It's been twenty-five minutes since you called me. Stop being dramatic. That's my department. Now tell me what's going on?"

June motioned to me to hop up onto the tabletop next to her so we could both "hide" behind the Daily Scoop paper.

"Okay, so here I was, minding my own business, searching for the ripest strawberries and the firmest rhubarb, and the next thing I know, I see a flash of red exactly the shade of Cliff's new girlfriend's hair disappear behind the vendor's barn. I automatically thought it must be Cliff and Sirena, so I started walking over to say good morning."

I rolled my eyes behind the paper. This sounded like June was suffering from a case of jealousy and using her instinct for investigation to stick her nose in places where it didn't belong.

June let out a huff. "I saw that eye roll. Anyhow, as I was walking over, I could see the shadows of two people on the grass behind the barn. They were clearly arguing, throwing their arms up in the air and gesturing like crazy, so I stopped. I kind of saw the whole thing like a puppet show in the shadows. A man grabbed her. She turned and slapped him across the face. The man raised his fist like he was going to hit her then turned toward where I was hiding and I had to run. I've been watching ever since, but I haven't seen anyone I recognize come out from around the barn. We need to go check it out."

"We are going to do no such thing. There is nothing to check out. You are going to pick up your bag of produce, sit your butt in my golf cart, and be very, very quiet all the way back home. Honestly, June, sometimes you're even too much for me."

"But, Francie, I'm sure it was her. She might need our help."

"Think about it. If she's been back there for twenty-five minutes, the only thing she might need is a blanket because she must be napping. Now, come on please. Let's go."

It's not like me to be the voice of reason, but for once I believed that June's imagination had taken a turn down a dark path.

"Okay, Francie, you win. It does sound a bit ridiculous when you say it out loud, but I'm not leaving until I know Sirena isn't sneaking around on Cliff and getting herself in trouble. Let's take a quick peek behind the barn. Humor me. If there's nothing suspicious there, we can leave."

I may not be an investigative journalist or a detective, but I do have a pretty good spidey-sense. And right now, the hairs on the back of my neck were standing at attention. Something was telling me nothing good would come of this. I also knew, however, that June would not let it go. She would investigate on her own if I refused to tag along, and who knows what she would get herself into. So against my better judgment, I got to my feet and followed her in the direction of the big weathered barn.

We were about fifty feet from the old building when June's phone began ringing out the Carly Simon classic "You're So Vain." There was no doubt in my mind about the identity of the person trying to reach her. She stopped and answered Cliff's call, and from what I gathered from her side of the conversation, it didn't sound like a social call.

While I waited for June to finish up, I wandered over to the section of the market where the artisan and crafts booths were grouped. I was pleased to see the Relaxed Crafts sign displayed on a nearby table under an attractive canopy, so I moseyed over to see what was new this season.

"Hi, John! I'm glad to see you haven't given up your hobby."

"Hi to you too, Francie! It's so good to see you again. I'd ask you how your winter was, but what's the point of that? The sun is shining and I've got lots of inventory thanks to my hobby. It's what kept me sane when we were stuck in the house during all those snow storms. The only trick is I have to be careful not to take on too many projects at once now that summer's here again."

"That's so true," I replied. "It's all about finding the right balance, isn't it?"

"Yes, and speaking of balance, I have something here I know you're going to like."

Not only was John a talented craftsman, he also had a real knack for sales. He directed my attention to a beautiful, monogrammed mahogany self-balancing wine bottle holder. It seemed to defy gravity; the bottle in the wood holder seemed to be floating perpendicular to the table.

"I've never seen anything like that. It's beautiful! Of course I'll be needing one."

"I have your address on file. I can ship it to your home. You haven't moved, have you?"

"No. Still in the same place. I'd like the darker stain and an 'E' for the monogram."

I was still carrying the newspaper I had picked up from our "hiding spot" but needed my free hand so I could locate my glasses and sign for my purchases. I was about to ask John to throw the paper away for me when I noticed an article circled several times in red ink. The headline read "Chicago Millionaire Philanthropist Dies In House Fire: Valuable Coin Collection Still Missing." I figured June must have been doing some digging for a new story while she was waiting for me to meet her so I tucked the paper into my bag, found my glasses and credit card, and signed for my purchase.

As John was handing back my credit card, June approached, disconnecting from her call.

"Well? What was that all about?"

"It was Cliff," she said, sounding exasperated.

"I gathered that. What did he want? Was he looking for Sirena?"

June looked a bit sheepish. "No. I could clearly hear a lady's voice giggling in the background. I mean, very clearly. It turns out that Cliff has been staying in a room at the same B&B where I was registered, and I'm assuming Sirena must have spent the night there with him."

Pulling at strands of her hair and clearing her throat, she continued. "Anyhow, this morning, the innkeeper made the connection between Cliff and me because the two of us had stayed there together on a few occasions. He mentioned that I had left the bed and breakfast but I hadn't checked out. He wanted to rent the room out, but wasn't sure what to do since I had left a few personal belongings in the room. Cliff said he would contact me and find out what my plans were and what was going on. I'm not sure why, but he ended up volunteering to take my things and make sure they were returned to me."

"That would never happen in the city. Islands certainly have their own set of rules. I'm assuming Cliff wasn't very happy about the task."

"You're right. He wasn't. He said he was planning to spend the whole weekend 'relaxing,' but that if he came back to the mainland, he would leave my bags with Steve at the guard booth."

"So, Sirena has been with him this whole morning?"

June was looking suitably embarrassed as she replied, "Yes. At least, it appears she was."

I knew from experience that June could take pouting to a whole new level, so I breathed a sigh of relief, thankful our snooping adventure was unexpectedly cancelled and changed the subject to whether or not I should buy a second floating wine holder for the condo. She knew what I was doing, gratefully took the easy out, and helped me select my second purchase.

A tap on my shoulder startled me into a quick turn, and I came within an inch of running smack dab into Roger Burns. "Oh, hi there, Roger. What are you doing way over here on the mainland this morning?"

"Sorry I startled you. I thought you saw me earlier over by the barn. I figured you were heading over to say hello, and I didn't want to be rude."

"I didn't see you. I was concentrating on finding June and got sidetracked by a little shopping. It's nice to see you though. Is Ruby here as well?"

"Uh, no she isn't. I had some business to take care of. Well, take care. See you soon."

June and I stared at Roger's back as he disappeared as quickly as he had arrived.

OUR RIDE BACK TO BEACON Pointe was sweetly uneventful.

By the time Hamm returned to the condo, laden with bags of nautical supplies, June and I were elbow deep in the kitchen, working on our respective dishes for the cookout later that evening. This was more like it: fresh ingredients from the market, Bloody Mary's in a pitcher, an assortment of snacks on a plate, and the island sounds from the stereo inviting us to find that lost shaker of salt. Hamm made himself comfortable on a stool at the kitchen counter, poured himself a drink, and fixed a snack. Finally, the mood had lightened up, and things were returning to a normal weekend pattern.

Hamm had chilled out and I was happy to discover he was in a talkative mood. "Honey, do you remember the Memorial Day excitement we had back when the kids were ten years old?"

"Do you mean the striking matches in the pocket excitement? How could I forget?"

"I know, right? We should write a book about the devilish shenanigans of pre-teens. On second thought, we probably shouldn't proudly announce and describe in detail all the wool they managed to pull over our eyes."

June swiveled her bar stool to face us. "Oh, this one I have got to hear."

I smiled, thinking back to the return trip home from our Memorial Day weekend ten years ago. We had spent three days swimming at the beach, playing in the park, and watching fireworks from the back of the boat and were all exhausted on our car ride back home. The twins were in the backseat carrying on with their usual antics: teasing, poking, and generally annoying each other. It was a typical ride home until smoke started filling the interior of the car and Ben yelled to pull over. Hamm swerved off the highway and Ben wasted no time jumping out of the car and proceeding to drop his shorts to the ground while running in circles and squealing. It turned out he had snuck some striking matches from the box by our grill in hopes of finding some sparklers or smoke bombs to claim for his own fireworks display. He never got around to using the matches for his intended purpose, thank goodness, but during their back seat scuffle, Ben wouldn't stop teasing Beth, so Beth punched him in the leg repeatedly, and the matches did what they were designed to do—they ignited. The rest is history. This put a whole new spin on the phrase, "Liar, liar pants on fire."

By the end of my rendition, June was laughing so hard she snorted. "How have I never heard that one before? I'm glad the kids were okay, but how long were they grounded for that little episode?"

"Let's just say, the yard looked really nice for the rest of the summer, compliments of Beth and Ben landscaping."

Chapter Thirteen

We arrived at the club around five o'clock. The double wide trailer that served as home to the yacht club sported a fresh coat of paint. The brass anchor fastened to the front of the clubhouse had been shined, and one of the green-thumbed members had planted red and white Impatiens in the mulched beds out front. Hamm and I walked around back to the kitchen entrance so I could drop off my pasta salad, adding it to the assortment of platters and dishes abundant with appetizers, desserts, and salads already covering the counters. While I arranged my plate among the other salads, Hamm scanned the tables until he located June's strawberry rhubarb pie. Relieved, he grinned and headed out the kitchen door to join a group of friends we hadn't seen since fall. Alone in the kitchen now, I heard sounds coming from the common area. Stepping away from the food, I peeked through the doorway and discovered the source. People were moving and rearranging furniture. I recognized several of my favorite vendors and local merchants setting up their wares on tables throughout the space. This was new and I liked it. What a great way to expose people to the unique and creative wares offered right here in town. I decided not to interfere with the setup, but as I was turning back to the food tables, I caught Sirena looking up from her display and offered her a smile and a thumbs up. I wasn't sure if she recognized me because she lowered her eyes and got back to her task. No matter. I was ready to join Hamm outside.

The party was gearing up. Fragrant smoke swirled up from the two gas grills on the back patio. Red, white, and blue lanterns glowed invitingly above the picnic tables overlooking the beach. Each table had been decorated with sand buckets sporting tiny American flags and patriotic pinwheels twirling in the breeze. I was excited to see one of my favorite summertime bands?the Rolling Hams?who were doing their sound check on the patio.

I was glad things worked out the way they had. Yacht club parties were always a good time, and the way the resort kept expanding and adding houses and pools and restaurants, our unimposing club, sitting on a prime piece of beachfront real estate, was likely on the verge of extinction. Most of the members, Hamm and I included, were determined to enjoy the facilities until we were chased out by bulldozers.

After our trip down memory lane earlier, I was aware of how much I wished our children were here with us this year. It's hard letting go so they could make their own memories. I hoped they were enjoying their camping trip to Hocking Hills. They had reconnected with some mutual friends from high school and decided to spend a few days together before resuming their separate paths.

"Hey Francie, over here!" I looked in the direction of the bar where I spotted June. In honor of Memorial Day, she wore a sequined red tank top, blue shorts and a headband with a large silver star. On her feet were silver wedge sandals, and her toenails were painted red with white stars decorating the center of each one. This latest outfit was one for the books, but true to form, she pulled it off. I wondered when she had time to change the streak in her hair from turquoise to royal blue. I must say, it brought out the color of her eyes.

My own patriotic ensemble was of a more classic variety. I chose my navy blue and white-striped maxi skirt, slit up the right side, and a solid navy V-neck top which showed off the curves I had worked on all winter. I was feeling pretty, and the red sandals I had on the night before were going to keep my tootsies cool and comfortable all night. I had twisted my hair into a loose ponytail, letting random strands curl around my face. Silver hoop earrings completed my outfit.

I ordered a glass of red wine at the bar, but before I could compliment June on her fashion sense, my attention was diverted to the big-screen TV inside the clubhouse. A crowd was gathering, and I stretched my neck to see what all the fuss was about. What I saw was Clifton Sterling's network rival, Linda Langley, delivering a breaking news update.

"The inferno completely destroyed a local family-owned boutique on picturesque Kelleys Island. Fire marshals are investigating the cause of the blaze. We don't have many details yet, but we will update this story for you as soon as we receive more information. Tune in at eleven."

Linda flashed her award-winning smile as images of Ruby's Treasure Chest—before and after the blaze—appeared on the screen. Seconds later, the newscast blinked forward to the next thirty-second disaster. June and I mirrored wide-open eyes and mouths and made a beeline for the bathroom to process this shocking news.

"We were just there! Poor Ruby. Poor Roger. I can't imagine who could have done this. Do you think it was an accident?"

We sucked in air at the same time and stared at each other.

June exhaled before asking, "Do you think Hamm knows something? Did he say anything to you last night? He must know something. Why else would he have been acting so strangely last night?"

My mind was reeling. I remembered my husband's torn, dirty clothes; that smoky, sweet odor that clung to him; and his strange behavior. His explanation for all these things had to be the truth. I believed him of course, but so much was happening I was having difficulty arranging the events into a cohesive picture. It felt like attempting to put together a jigsaw puzzle blindfolded. There were pieces missing but I couldn't know what they were or where they belonged.

"Come on, Francie. Let's go back outside." June's warm, steady hand was on my elbow, guiding me out the door and back to the party where everything looked natural and unexceptional.

I scanned the crowd for Hamm, trying to ignore the sense of dread rising like a yeasty loaf in my stomach. I needed to see him, put my arms around him, look into his eyes. I needed to talk to him.

"There he is, June. I need to find out what's going on. Stay here."

"No way I'm standing by and missing the scoop. Let's go."

Hamm was on the beach, staring across the water in the direction of Kelleys Island. He looked like a stone statue silhouetted against the marble sky. Detective Morgan was walking toward him. June and I made our way through the crowd of friends and club acquaintances who were busy trying to get the scoop on the fire. Snippets of theories and speculations brushed by us as we kept our course toward the two men.

I was about to call out a greeting but changed my mind and held my tongue when I heard Morgan's voice.

"I'll stay in touch. Don't make any plans to leave town for a while."

Hamm appeared calm and relaxed when Morgan turned back toward him. "Hey, do you happen to have a light? This time I saved my daily indulgence for tonight." He casually pointed a cigar in Hamm's direction.

"Sorry Jack, my lighter went missing some time last night, probably when we were at the Island House. Seems like I've had problems holding on to that thing lately."

Morgan narrowed his eyes but said nothing. He stood for a few seconds without moving, then turned back toward the club and walked in our direction. We weren't exactly spying, or even eavesdropping, but nevertheless I felt like we'd been caught red-handed.

"Good evening ladies. It's a great night for a party." He gave June an appraising look from her headband right down to her painted toenails. I wouldn't have been surprised if the sand under her feet turned to glass from all of the heat emanating between them. "I wish I could stay for the festivities, but duty calls. Night, June." I thought I heard him humming as he walked away.

June stood melted to the sand, watching Jack leave, but I made a beeline for Hammond. "Oh, honey, what was that all about? Was Jack questioning you? What did he want? What did you say? Where is he going now? Does he think...?"

Hamm placed his strong hands on my shoulders and looked me in the eyes. "First of all, Francesca, breathe."

I gulped a mouthful of air and waited. He glanced at June, still standing a few paces off then directed his gaze back to my face. "Listen, everything is fine. Morgan is simply doing his job. He wondered if we saw or heard anything out of the ordinary last night. That's all. Just routine."

"So he told you about Ruby's? Can you believe it? We caught the newscast at the club. I'm still in shock."

Hamm softly repeated, "Just routine, just doing his job." I wasn't sure if he was trying to convince me or himself.

"Come on. Let's go back to the party. I could use a drink."

I looked back toward the partygoers and replied, "I couldn't agree more."

June followed us up the beach but when we reached the club, she veered off toward a trio of friends on the patio. Hamm and I made our way to the bar where he ordered a double Jack on ice and a glass of red wine for me.

"Hey, Hamm, I see your wish finally came true. You've been saying for years that you were planning night maneuvers to get rid of the evil red door and everything behind it."

"Good job, buddy! You've done all of us husbands a favor and saved us all tons of cash."

The ribbing was coming from all around us. "Hey, Francie, I guess you brought home one too many of those red bags from Ruby's."

"What was it that sent him over the edge? Was it one more bead for your bracelet or another serving dish? Was it worth it?"

Hamm was not impressed. He finished his drink in two long sips and set his glass on the bar. "Come on Francie, let's get out of here," he said between clenched teeth as he pulled me toward the parking lot. That dough ball in my stomach was rising to become a whole bakery shelf of dread.

Despite the tension radiating from my husband, the mood all around us was festive. The band began strumming the first chords of "Brown Eyed Girl," and people started migrating toward the dance floor and swaying to the beat. Conversations became louder and more animated. The guys tried to one-up each other with their fish tales and upgrades they'd added to their boats over the winter. They never got tired of hearing themselves talk about who had the biggest or cleanest or fastest boat in the marina.

The ladies' conversations leaned more toward who lost or gained weight over the winter; who went on the coolest vacations; literary fiction versus romance novels; and which recipes were bound for glory at this summer's cookouts. The party was in full swing.

"Come on, Hamm." I squeezed his hand and steered him away from the exit and onto the edge of the dance floor. "How about just one dance? Please?"

He looked down at my sad puppy face, then out toward the parking lot. Sad puppy face wins every time. He was tense at first, but once the lead singer belted out the chorus to our song, our hips were moving in sync, and like everyone around us, we were swaying to the Van Morrison classic. My skirt floated gently around me as he spun me in a quick turn, dipped me in a grand gesture, and planted a kiss right on my lips for all to see. When the song was over, both of us were a bit flushed, and Hamm seemed much more himself.

"Thanks for that, my brown-eyed girl. You always bring a smile to my face, even when I'm trying my hardest to perfect my frown."

"Even though this hasn't been the perfect start to our first weekend back, you always say a bad day at the beach is still better than a good day at home. I've always liked that saying."

"There is that."

Hamm's phone rang and after checking the caller display, he excused himself and walked around to the side of the building to take the call. There I was, feeling awkward and alone on the dance floor when June rushed up and stopped in front of me.

"Oh. My. Goodness. Francie, have you tried the buffalo dip or the fiery grilled shrimp yet? And did you see the vendors display? What a great idea to have them all here at the party so members can shop and place orders without skipping a beat. It's a win-win don't you think?"

June popped a shrimp in her mouth with one hand and took my elbow in her other, guiding me toward the clubhouse where, according to her, bliss awaited.

"Hang on a minute. I'm waiting for Hamm to finish a call, then we can all go."

"Really, Francie? Who is he talking to? And did I hear you correctly because I think you just said you wanted to wait for Hamm so he could do some shopping with us."

"Um. I guess that did sound odd. Let's go inside. But he does like to eat and we have to pass through the kitchen to get to the displays. I'm sure he could find a way to amuse himself."

June borrowed one of Hamm's comebacks, "There is that."

Once inside, I saw she was right. This looked like a win-win to me. I was surprised at how quickly the local shopkeepers had set up their displays while I was arranging my food in the kitchen. I stopped in front of the shrimp plate for a sample. June breezed by me heading for the vendor displays.

I was still chewing when Hamm strode through the door looking not at all like a man on vacation. "We need to go, Francie. It's been one thing after another this weekend. I'm sorry."

And just like that, everything changed.

Sometimes you just know when there's no point in arguing. This was one of those. I stepped away from the food table and got a glimpse of June standing in front of Sirena's eye-catching display. They were chatting and smiling and June had a box of chocolates in her hand. I tried to get her attention but was blocked from her view by a tall, handsome man holding a steaming cup of coffee. I waved in her direction unsure whether or not she had seen me.

On our way back to the condo, Hamm informed me he had to return home the next morning. He had to take care of some business that came up while we were trying to relax and enjoy our weekend. His partner was unreachable, so it was up to him to sort out the mess one of the interns made while filing a brief. Whatever.

My trip to paradise was turning into a bust. My husband was behaving strangely; I had to leave the party early and miss all the great food, drinks, and dancing; and not least by any means, Ruby's Treasure Chest was now a smoldering pile of ashes in a parking lot. Starting tomorrow, June and I would be alone for the rest of the holiday weekend. I switched between worry and anger and finally decided there wasn't much point to either. I vowed to make the best of things, come what may.

Chapter Fourteen

Back at the condo, everything was quiet. All our neighbors must have called it an early night after a long day at the beach or were out enjoying their own holiday gatherings. The front porch light was on and Hamm unlocked the door and shut it behind us like he was trying to keep the outside world from invading our last precious haven of peace and quiet. I slipped off my sandals and kicked them over to the entrance rug. For some reason, the house felt gloomy, so I turned on some lamps. I also decided to flip the switch on our electric fireplace in an attempt to chase away the chilly mood.

Hamm settled into the deep cushions of the sofa and rubbed the back of his neck with both hands. I went into the kitchen, uncorked a bottle of wine and poured two glasses. I'd come back for a bag of chips and some salsa in case Hamm felt like eating something. It wasn't June's homemade pie, but it would have to do.

"Here you go, honey. Let's make a toast to resolving work problems so you can get back here, and we can make a fresh start of our weekend."

Hamm's response was a low snore. I guess the day had done him in. I set one glass on the coffee table and raised the other. "Well, here's to me, I guess. Salud!"

I sat next to Hamm and put my feet on the table. I almost dropped my glass when my purse began vibrating with June's ringtone on the floor beside me. I tried to be quiet as I leaned over the arm of the sofa to rummage through the bottomless jumble of necessities. I got my hands on the device right before it was about to switch over to voicemail. What could be so important that she felt the need to call me so soon?

"Hello? June? What's up?"

"Ffffrrrrrrrrrn, issss me."

"Huh? Who is this? Is that you June?"

"Issssss me. I neeeeee yooooo. Urrrrrryyyy."

"What the heck, June? Are you drunk? I haven't even been gone an hour. What happened?" The only response I got was silence. The line had gone dead, but I continued to speak into the receiver. "What now? This weekend keeps getting weirder by the hour." Talking to myself wasn't helping, so I put my sandals back on, grabbed my purse and the golf cart key, and scribbled a hurried note for Hamm in case he woke up.

I reached the club in record time, the strange call from June weighing heavily on my mind. The party was still going strong. People were mingling near the bar and picking at the leftover desserts. Sadly, I noticed one of my diabetic friends savoring the last piece of June's strawberry rhubarb pie. I approached a small group of ladies gathered near the dance floor swaying to the music. "Hey, Lisa. Have you seen June around? I think she might have had too much to drink. She called me, and I could hardly understand what she was saying. I think she needed a ride back to the dock."

"Oh hey, Francie! Come have a drink with us. She was here for a while but I haven't seen her since she went out to the beach."

"Why was she going out to the beach? Was she alone?"

"You know June. She saw some cute guy with a dog out by the breakwall and said she had to talk to him real quick. I'm sure she was interested in more than talking though, if you know what I mean. So what are you drinking?"

"Sorry, Lisa, it's been a long day. I just came back to pick June up. I've got to get back to the condo. I left Hamm asleep there."

"Suit yourself! Good luck finding Junie. Last I saw her she was over there." She pointed toward the beach.

"Thanks, Lisa. Have fun."

I started walking toward the lake in the direction Lisa had pointed. The light from the moon was minimal, and it became harder to see as I got farther away from the party. Hopefully, I wasn't on another wild goose chase. I was starting to get crabby after the day's ups and downs. I needed to get a good night's sleep and start fresh tomorrow.

"June! Hey, June, are you out here?" I was halfway down the beach and nearing the breakwall and still no sign of my friend. I decided to go to the edge of the water where the limestone jutted out into the lake. If June didn't turn up, then I guess it was a good possibility she had found herself a handsome man to take care of her. Maybe Detective Morgan had come back. She would be safe and in good hands if she was with him.

I heard a low growl and noticed movement in the shadows up ahead. "June? Is that you? Come on, you're the one who called me out here, so let's go. I'll take you back to the condo with me and you can sleep this one off. I might even throw in some aspirin and a cup of coffee. June?"

Something furry brushed up against my leg and I let out a sharp scream. The next thing I knew I was lying on my back in the sand being slobbered upon by some furry creature. "What the ...? Help me! Help! Get off of me! "

"Gunner, heel!" A commanding voice sounded out of the dark. The fuzzy, licking monster jumped off me and sat at attention on the ground by my feet. I was struggling to sit up when the figure of a man blocked the light of the moon completely. He reached out his hand and helped me to my feet.

"Sorry, ma'am. That's my dog Gunner. He gets a little over-excited sometimes and forgets his manners." He cleared his throat like he wasn't used to talking much more than a few words at a time. "I guess I'm lacking in the manners department too. My name's Michael. Are you by any chance Francie?"

"Yes?" His question startled me and my answer came out sounding more like a question as well.

"I know your friend June. We met last summer and have spoken several times since then. My buddy Gunner here is a big fan of hers. Right now, she's sleeping it off over there by the rocks. Gunner and I were sitting out here on the breakwall listening to the music from the party when, out of nowhere, here comes June. I knew right away it was her by the clothes she's wearing. We spoke briefly at the vendor display inside and she was perfectly fine. She had purchased a box of chocolates from the owner of the new boutique and offered me one. I came out here right after that, so it couldn't have been more than fifteen minutes when she showed up bobbing and weaving and stumbling all over the place. I went over to see if I could help her. When I got to her, she was mumbling about mermaids and detectives and Francie and cheese? I couldn't make any sense of what she was trying to tell me. Then she passed out. I checked she was breathing regularly and didn't have any injuries, and I made sure there wasn't anything near her that could harm her. I don't own a cell phone so I was on my way up to the clubhouse to see about getting some help when you showed up.

"Oh no, that makes no sense. No way she was drunk." I brushed as much sand off my behind as I could while I half-stumbled, half-ran over to the lumpy shadow near the end of the breakwall. June was curled up on her side with an army jacket folded under her head. The look on her face was angelic. Her breathing was strong and regular. That being said, she wasn't going anywhere without assistance. She was out cold.

"Michael, thank you so much for helping June, but I'm going to need to ask you for another favor. There's no way I can get her back to my condo by myself. Could you help me get her in the golf cart and ride back with me and help me get her inside?"

Without a word, Michael picked June up like she was a rag doll, carried her across the sand to where I had left my ride, and laid her gently across the back seat. I picked up the jacket, and Gunner hopped right up beside her and sat at attention. Michael slid into the front passenger seat and stared straight ahead. When I handed him his jacket, he thanked me so quietly, he might have simply been clearing his throat again.

The man was intimidating, but he had a friendly dog and he smelled nice.

SUNDAY MORNING THE weather was right in line with the gloomy tone of the recent events. Gray clouds hung outside the bedroom window like damp wool. Hammond got up at the crack of dawn and gathered his things for his return home. "Francesca, what on earth is June doing in the guest room?"

"Um, she had a little too much to drink last night at the party and called me shortly after you fell asleep asking me to pick her up. I drove the golf cart down to the club and brought her back here while you were still asleep. I didn't want her to be alone in case she woke up and didn't remember where she was."

"Typical June."

I felt bad. It was too early for Hamm to be mumbling under his breath about June's behavior. I couldn't imagine what he would think if I filled him in on all the details from the previous night. I thought it best to leave that information out for now until I could get the whole story from June. Maybe by the time I relayed the events to Hamm, it would be just another "Nutty June" story to laugh about. Right now, I was not finding anything funny about last night's turn of events.

Hamm pulled me in for a hug and a quick kiss before he placed his empty coffee cup in the sink and picked up his bag to head out.

"I love you, Francesca. Please stay close to home and don't go poking around into other people's business. Maybe you and June could just hang out on the deck today, do some reading, get some sun, that kind of thing? I'd ask you to come back with me, but I know that would be useless. So please, promise me."

I pulled a cardigan over my pajama top, trying to chase away the chill in the room. The prospect of getting any sun today looked wildly remote at this point. I thought Hamm was going to say something else, but he just looked at me with an expression that was not covered in my Theater's Handbook of Facial Expressions and Emotions.

"Of course I promise. Why would I want to interfere with the authorities? I want them to find out who did this terrible thing to our friends as soon as possible." This was mostly true, but just to be safe, my fingers were crossed behind my back.

"All right then. Don't let June talk you into doing anything stupid, and make sure she didn't break any laws last night. I love you."

"Always the attorney—love you too, hon. Call or text me when you get back, and be careful."

Before the door swung shut behind Hamm, I was opening the door to the guest bedroom to check on June. I needed to find out what happened to her last night, but it didn't look like I'd be getting any information out of her for a while. She was curled up under the covers, and just like last night, she was breathing deeply, a look of angelic sweetness on her face. It was still early, so I decided to brew another pot of coffee and do some research on the Internet. Maybe I could figure out what, if not who, had caused her bizarre behavior last night. About two hours and four cups of coffee into my digital foray, I had begun to formulate a hypothesis. Her extreme behavior was not induced by alcohol and I was convinced it was caused by a quick-acting agent June would never have purposely ingested or been exposed to. I didn't know who would want to hurt her, but I was determined to find out.

June walked bleary-eyed out of the bathroom and plopped down at the kitchen table. Her face was scrubbed clean and she was wearing green camouflage cargo pants with a lacy white T-shirt that she must have found in one of Beth's drawers. In spite of her fragile condition, she still managed to look great.

"Francie, what happened last night? Everything is all mixed up in my head, and I'm having a hard time deciding what is real and what I dreamt. The last thing I can remember for sure is ordering a drink with Lisa, then running into the club to powder my nose in case Jack decided to make a reappearance. He is so mysterious. I wouldn't mind finding out what makes him tick. Anyway, I went back to hang out with Lisa and had finished about half of my drink when I saw Michael and Gunner out by the breakwall. At least, I think that's what happened. I thought if I brought him a piece of my pie, maybe I could get Michael to open up to me a little bit. I don't even care about getting a story out of him anymore. I just think he's probably a great guy with some trust issues, so I wrapped up a piece and headed out there. The next thing I remember is waking up in your guest room. I know I didn't have that much to drink."

"Oh my gosh, June. I don't know what happened. I got a call from you, but I couldn't understand a thing you said. You were speaking gibberish. I think you said you needed help. I figured you met up with some of your friends and had too much to drink. I did think it was strange though because not enough time had passed for you to get intoxicated. It couldn't have been more than forty minutes. I went back to the club to pick you up, but I couldn't find you anywhere. Lisa told me you headed down to the beach so I went looking. The next thing I knew I was being slobbered to death by a dog and meeting your mystery friend Michael. He said you were stumbling all over and talking about mermaids and cheese or something. Then you passed out."

"Francie, do you think someone put something in my drink?"

"It seems plausible but who would do that? And better yet, why? I don't think you've created any mortal enemies on the island. Is there something you're not telling me?"

"What? Of course not! I'm just trying to come up with some sort of explanation for all of this. Do you have any aspirin? I have a splitting headache."

I got the aspirin bottle from the cupboard, filled a glass of water, and placed both on the table. "I don't know, June. You were passed out cold when I got there. Michael had to carry you to my golf cart. He rode back with me and helped me get you inside and into the bedroom, which is something considering the way you say he avoids people. Thank God Hamm sleeps like the dead, or he would have had a heart attack when he saw that hunky GI Joe roaming around the condo."

"Dang! Why did I have to be out cold while Prince Charming was carrying me around? Did he kiss me to see if I was under the spell of an evil queen?"

"No, and there were no dwarves waiting in the wings to celebrate either. Come on, June, get serious."

"Sorry, you know me better than anyone. I try to make light of things when I'm scared, and believe me, right now, I'm scared. All I can tell you is that I was fine one minute and the next I was waking up in your guest bedroom. Everything in between is gone. If something fishy isn't going on then my name isn't Juniper Julia Augusta."

"I believe you. There's no reason to go getting technical."

I knew I had to get June's mind off the mystery from last night for now, and the best plan I could come up with was breakfast. All of this stuff would need to be processed, but first things first. I unwrapped a couple of cheese Danishes from the local bakery and set them on the kitchen table with a bowl of fruit and a steaming cup of coffee. June dug in and was acting more like herself within minutes.

I was already over-caffeinated, so I passed on more coffee and settled in on the chair across from my best friend. "Do you think you're up for a trip back over to Kelleys to check on Ruby today?"

"Absolutely. But I can't believe Hamm would be okay with you wanting to go back to the island and talk to Ruby and Roger."

"I may have forgotten to mention that small detail. Right now we should work our way through all of these stranger-than-fiction events and hopefully unravel the cause of your blackout. Are you sure you feel up to it?"

"I have a headache, but I think the aspirin is kicking in. The coffee and food are helping. I was a little wobbly on my feet earlier, but I'll be fine and the fresh air will do me good. I only wish I could remember what happened."

"That's good because the next ferry leaves in about an hour, and it will take us at least twenty minutes to get to the ferry dock. We'll have to take my old Saturn. The golf cart got a flat tire right when we pulled into the drive last night. I guess I've abused it lately. I probably ran over a nail or something driving back and forth through all the new home construction around here. I hope the car has gas in it—heck, I hope it starts!"

It did. My old clunker made it all the way into town without stalling. We pulled into the ferry lot next to the Dairy Dock ice cream and hot dog stand with no minutes to spare, which in this case was probably a good thing because I have no willpower when it comes to their famous fresh strawberry sundaes, even right after breakfast. The damp morning breeze raised goosebumps on my arms, and I felt a tingle on the back of my neck that I told myself was due to the weather. After purchasing our tickets, we made our way up the gangplank and onto the Shirley Irene. We practically had the ferry to ourselves since most of the vacationers were already where they planned to be for the holiday weekend, so we stood inside the center cabin, out of the chilly air, and watched the rolling gray waves through the window. The rhythmic sound of the engines reminded me of the steady beat of a strong heart.

Chapter Fifteen

Twenty minutes later, the ferry docked the municipal pier. We disembarked and headed across the street, to the Village Pump, a local favorite restaurant open year round and famous for their perch and Brandy Alexanders. Here we could fortify ourselves for the day ahead. We ordered a basket of cheese sticks and a pitcher of hot, black coffee. It was way too early for cocktails, but the coffee was just right on this drizzly morning.

"Before we stop at Ruby's, do you mind if we make a detour over to the Island House and see if anyone turned in Hamm's lighter? I know it's out of our way, but he was pretty upset about misplacing it. I had it engraved with his initials and a small sentiment for our fifteenth wedding anniversary, and he's been using it for over five years now. It's weird that he misplaced it twice in the past two days. He's usually not prone to losing things. That's my department."

June licked the last crumbs off her fingers while I fished around in my voluminous handbag until I found some crumpled bills to pay for our order. It was my turn, since June had paid for our ferry tickets. Back outside, we walked to the end of the block, turned left, and continued down Division

Street to the Island House. It wasn't open yet, but we spotted the hostess who was setting up the patio and bar for the day.

"Excuse me, can I ask a favor? Could you please check your lost and found and look for a gold lighter with an engraved inscription?" She was nice enough to stop her prep and check the lost and found box, but unfortunately, Hamm's lighter was not among the misplaced items.

She held up a pretty silver sandal and remarked, "I never can figure out how someone loses one shoe, especially one with a heel."

Our heads all turned at the same time when the handsome detective, Jack Morgan, strode up to the bar. June hooked her thumbs in the top pockets of her cargo pants and batted her long eyelashes in his direction. "Hi there! The restaurant isn't open yet, and the bar doesn't serve alcohol until noon. You can't be ready for a drink yet, can you?"

"I'm a hot-shot detective, you know. Maybe I'm just out investigating where the prettiest ladies on the island spend their mornings." Although he had used the term "ladies," Morgan was directing his uncharacteristically light-hearted comment right at June whose cheeks were turning a rosy pink.

Megan, our helpful hostess, had disappeared. When she came back out to the patio, she was carrying a large, white to-go bag and a Styrofoam cup of steaming black coffee.

"Thanks, Megan. I appreciate your accommodating me."

Did he just say, "accommodating me?" I noticed June was giving a second, more discriminating look to the helpful hostess. She was probably half my age, decorated with several strategically placed, artful tattoos, and her long ballerina legs were tan and smooth. June's antennae were seriously twitching.

My friend had managed to reposition herself so she was right next to Morgan, her nose centimeters from his food. "You must really rate around here. That smells delicious, and I know the kitchen isn't open yet."

Megan casually replied, "Oh, we've been making Jack a special-order Reuben to-go every weekday morning, and a ham and Swiss on rye on Sunday, since a week after he moved to the island. It's nice to have a professional around to 'serve and protect,' if you know what I mean."

Now it was the detective's turn to blush. Morgan's cheeks flushed red (which had the effect of making him even more adorable if that was possible). A strange coughing sound escaped from June's throat. She was shooting an evil eye in Megan's direction now. There were way too many hormones zinging around here for this early in the day.

"So, Detective"—I decided it was time to change the subject—"have you made any progress on the cause of the fire?"

"Well, I was hoping to talk to the two of you today. Do you have a minute to sit down and help me get a few things straight about Friday night? I'm sure Megan wouldn't mind if we have a quick cup of coffee out here on the patio."

Jack pulled a chair out for June, and once I realized that was as far as his chivalry was going to go, I took a seat across from the two of them. We sat around the table in the same seats we had occupied Friday, only this time it was starting to feel less like a friendly gathering and more like an interrogation. Morgan gave me a long stare. Why did he constantly make me feel like I was guilty of something? I refused the offer of coffee when Megan brought a pot and three cups to our table. I was feeling jittery enough. June held her cup out so Detective

Morgan could fill it and for a moment, I felt as if I were intruding on something. She took a long drink, never taking her eyes off his face, and sat on the edge of her seat in anticipation of learning more about the investigation.

I figured I might as well break the spell. "So what do you need to know about, Jack? We were all here together that night, so I don't know what we could possibly help you with."

"We weren't all here the entire evening if you recall. How was Hammond when you returned to your boat that night?"

The question was directed at me, and I felt like a deer caught in headlights. Hamm certainly was upset and filthy when he returned, but why would Morgan be concerned about that?

"He was fine." When I heard my own voice in answer to his question, it did not sound very convincing.

"So nothing struck you as unusual at all that night?"

"Well, Francie and I did identify those minnow bandits. That was pretty unusual." June came to my rescue with her quick answer. I thanked her in my mind and waited for the next impossible question to be posed.

Morgan was rubbing his jaw and looking at each of us in turn. "We do appreciate the information you gave us to nail those minnow thieves. They've been a thorn in the side of the marina owners since last season, but thanks to your detailed descriptions, the police were able to identify them easily. Those two losers won't be bothering our locals for a long time. It turns out the boat they were using didn't belong to them, so we added grand theft to their rap sheet on top of stealing and illegal sale of stolen property. Once again, thank you. It was smart of you to get the OH numbers off the boat."

"We do what we can," June answered as if it were part of her daily routine to bring lawbreakers to justice.

"But back to Friday night, I have one more question about the fire investigation. Has Hammond ever been inside Ruby's store or in her upstairs office?"

I stared mutely at our interrogator. Thankfully, June hadn't also lost her voice. "Of course he hasn't been in Ruby's office. That would require his walking through the entire store past shelves and racks of girlie things, all for sale. Besides, what possible reason would he have for going up there?"

That was my thought exactly. I found my voice. "Why are you wasting time investigating my husband's smoking and shopping habits when you should be looking for some criminal who is going around starting fires?"

Morgan reached into the pocket of his jacket and pulled out a sealed plastic bag marked evidence. Inside the bag, I could clearly see my husband's treasured, engraved, missing lighter. "Right now, we are focusing on identifying the charred remains of a victim found in Ruby's attic office. I can't share any specifics of the case, but I think you can imagine what finding Hamm's lighter at the scene implies. I need to talk to him as soon as possible. Is he back at the condo? I've been trying to reach him there without any luck."

I didn't want to answer that question. It seemed like everything I said was making Hamm look more suspicious. I figured it wouldn't bode well to lie to a detective though, especially one that my best friend had the hots for. Besides, Hamm didn't do anything wrong. The sooner he talked to Morgan, the sooner this misunderstanding could be cleared up and the real criminal would be caught. "He went back home to his office this morning. There was a problem with one of his upcoming cases. I'm sure if you leave a message with his secretary, he will get back to you as soon as he arrives."

"Thanks for your time, ladies. I did enjoy seeing you this morning June, even if it is under these circumstances. I don't like the fact that Hammond has left, and I'd appreciate it if you and your friend would keep as far away from the situation as possible. That is, unless, you think of something that might help this investigation move forward. Here's my card and my cell phone number. Call me if you remember anything."

June blushed as she took his card and we watched him stride across the patio and out to the street.

I slumped farther into my chair. I needed Hammond's confident voice to tell me everything would be fine. It had been less than two hours since we were together, but I was feeling vulnerable. I located my cell phone in my bag and dialed Hamm's number. No answer. Well, he was probably still driving. I'd give him enough time to get to his office and try again later.

By the time I stashed my phone back in my bag, June was pacing on the sidewalk in front of the bar, so I joined her in walking back toward the marina, covering the short distance to Ruby's house. Her historic stone house stood right beside the gaping, charred lot that just yesterday was her pride and joy. The Burns house was constructed of thick gray stone that had weathered decades of nature's fury and still possessed all of its original charm. The structure was sturdy and had withstood the fire, but I could only imagine what the smoke had done to the interior of the house. Where would you begin to clean something like this up?

We began our walk in silence, but that didn't last. June and I talked over each other, our tongues tripping over our words, sentences jumbling together, trying to find a speck of sanity among all this craziness. Questions about a nameless victim killed in the fire, police speculation about Hamm, the missing lighter, and a criminal lurking about on our vacation island buzzed around our heads like a swarm of killer bees.

We spotted Ruby in her front yard. She had a red bandana tied around her hair, her face was smudged, and her clothes were wrinkled. She was shaking out a rug like she was wrestling with it for her life.

As soon as I saw her, the tears that had threatened to spill over my eyes made good on their promise. "Oh, Ruby! I'm so sorry! This is awful. There's nothing left!"

The three of us connected in a spontaneous group hug. When we separated, Ruby looked at me with an expression I didn't recognize. I needed a new handbook.

"Thank you, girls. Your concern means a lot to me. People have been so kind and helpful. Sirena came by and offered to help me sift through the rubble in the store. I wasn't sure what I was trying to accomplish at first. I think maybe Sirena was trying to distract me." Ruby looked around before lowering her voice to just above a whisper. "I probably shouldn't be saying anything. I don't know how much information the police want shared."

"What is it, Ruby?" After hearing this, there was no way I was going to simply drop the whole thing.

"About an hour into the clean-up project, the firemen came down from the attic and said we had to leave because the whole building was now a crime scene. There was someone up there.

They couldn't tell if it was a man or a woman. The victim was so badly burned." I have no idea who it is or how anyone could have been inside."

Detective Morgan had mentioned that a body was found in the attic, but hearing it again, this time from Ruby, made it all the more terrible. Who was it? Why was Hamm's lighter there? Where was Hamm?

Ruby gave me that odd look again. "Francie, I couldn't help it. I had to tell him."

"Tell him what? What are you talking about, Ruby?"

"Detective Morgan was asking over and over if there was anyone who had anything against us or wanted to hurt us. I kept saying no, no, no. I wanted him to stop badgering me, so I told him about how your husband would never come into the store, and how he had mentioned a few times how his life would be so much easier if my store would disappear. I'm sorry, Francie! I just wanted him to stop asking me questions."

That explained the looks Ruby had been giving me. "Of course Hammond had nothing to do with this! He may hate shopping, but he thinks the world of you and Roger. And he is absolutely not capable of anything this horrible!"

"I didn't say he did anything." Ruby's terse reply took me by surprise, but then I remembered what she had just been through, what she was still going through, and decided to let it go. I looked to June to help me get out of this, but she was nowhere to be seen.

"So what can I do to help? Do you or Roger need anything?"

"We're fine for now. We'll probably grab some clothes if we can find anything that doesn't smell like smoke and head over to the hotel for now. The whole house will need to be professionally cleaned. Everything smells awful."

"COME ON, FRANCIE, WE'VE got to get going. We'll be in touch soon, Ruby. Take care!"

June was back beside me and anxious to leave.

"What the heck was that all about? Where did you disappear to?"

June kept looking over her shoulder as she dragged me away from the yard where Ruby still stood, bandana askew, rug still in hand. June was agitated. She explained to me that, as usual, she was feeling antsy, so she had headed around to the back of the house to see if there was anything she could do to help. She came upon Roger Burns in the backyard, deep in conversation with a man she didn't recognize. Before she had the chance to call out a greeting, she overheard the words "fire, money, and merchandise."

"I kept to the shadows until the shady-looking man mumbled something to Roger and left on foot by way of the alley on the side of the house. Then I made my way back. Francie, something's going on, and it's not good. I think Roger might be in trouble."

I looked over my shoulder at Ruby as I tripped along beside June. Roger was standing next to her, and they were deep into a heated exchange. Before I turned back, Ruby pointed her finger at me and shook her head. For a nanosecond, our eyes met. Then she turned away, and she and Roger headed toward their house and out of view. The stranger June spoke of was nowhere to be seen.

Chapter Sixteen

"Francie, I think the best thing we can do to help Ruby and probably Hamm is to follow the man who was talking to Roger and see where he goes. It looks like he's involved in something, and it doesn't look good."

Hamm's words kept running through my mind. "Don't go poking around into other people's business. Promise me." Then there was the detective's admonishment. "Keep as far away from the situation as possible." I couldn't help myself. My friends were in trouble so I ignored both of these reasonable voices and went with June's spidey-sense.

"Okay, June, I'm with you on this one, but if we're going to follow this guy, we'll need transportation. I guess we could rent a couple bikes from the kiosk in town. Did you see what kind of car he was driving?"

"He was on foot, but he was fast. He went north."

When we got to the rental kiosk, there was no one manning the rental station, so we did the next best thing?improvise. I fished a magic marker and an unsent postcard from my trip to Idaho three years ago out of my bag. I scrawled a quick IOU on the card and held it in front of our honest, smiling faces to snap a selfie with my smartphone.

Next, I friended the rental company on Facebook and uploaded the IOU picture to its business page. Feeling very responsible, we selected a tandem bicycle and hopped on (because "borrowing" only one bike was better than riding off with two) and pedaled in the direction June saw the man heading.

We caught a glimpse of the stranger as we headed to the north side of the island. He was now driving a golf cart, which he must have had parked somewhere down the road from Ruby's. It was easy to keep him in sight because whenever the sun peaked out from behind a dismal cloud, it glinted on the dime-sized diamond in his left ear and magnified the shine coming from his slick, black ponytail. Trying to look like incognito holiday tourists, we pedaled behind him at a respectable distance. We weren't worried about losing him since the road we were on basically was a big circle ringing the island. We rode past the island cemetery, Glacial Grooves, and the state park. As we neared an abandoned fishing dock and dilapidated warehouse located in a sparsely populated stretch of land, we began to wonder if perhaps we were wasting our time on this guy, barking up the wrong tree.

The man in the golf cart came to a stop next to a windowless white van parked beside the old warehouse, far back from the road. We secured the tandem bike in a stand of trees that kept us well out of sight but allowed us a pretty good view of the mystery man. He was wearing a black leather jacket and black boots. His wrap-around black sunglasses completed his creeper/biker/criminal outfit. While we stood watching the scene, June told me once more what she witnessed behind

Ruby's house. I still couldn't wrap my mind around what I was hearing.

"Do you think Roger could be involved in any of this? Who is this guy? And what was Roger doing talking to him? Are you sure you heard the guy say 'fire?'"

The man in black stopped beside the golf cart and looked from left to right. I held my breath when he turned his head right in our direction. I was regretting my decision to wear my orange blouse with the glittery flowers across the chest. It was one of my summer favorites and complimented my tan walking shorts perfectly, but right now I felt like a glow-in-the-dark target. June, on the other hand, looked like she had dressed specifically for this occasion. The man in black finally went back to whatever it was he was doing. To be on the safe side, I pulled my emergency sweater out of my bag and wrapped myself in its beige comfort. June jabbed me in the ribs just as I was knotting the sweater's belt around my waist.

"Look, Francie! What is he doing? We need to find out what's going on over there."

The man was unloading cardboard boxes from the van and carrying them into the old warehouse.

I bent down and retrieved my phone from the pile of leaves it had landed in when I was looking for my sweater. It gave me an idea. I waited for the man to come out of the warehouse, and as he stepped toward the van, I located my phone's camera app and zoomed in on the man's face. I saw the jagged scar running from his right ear down across his throat and disappearing beneath his T-shirt collar. The phone was shaking in my hands as I made sure the flash was turned off and snapped pictures of the man, the van, and the warehouse. My feeling all of this must be connected to the fire and the victim in Ruby's attic was growing stronger.

June pulled her own phone out of the cargo pocket on her right thigh. She was much more poised under pressure than I was, and she began systematically photographing the scene as if it was a part of a feature story she was working on.

We watched as he carried six more boxes into the abandoned warehouse. When he was finished, he drove the golf cart behind the building and covered it with a tarp. After one more sweeping glance of the surroundings, he got into the van and headed toward town.

I stared at my phone. Once again, I felt an overwhelming need to talk to Hamm. What the heck was I doing hiding behind trees taking pictures of a creepy stranger? I hit the speed dial button for my husband's cell phone and waited. I was told by an annoying computer voice to "please enjoy the ringtone while my party was being reached." I did not enjoy the music and my party was not reached.

"Where are you, dammit?" Screaming at my phone brought no response from it.

June gently pried the phone from my hand and looked at the number on the screen. "What's the matter, Francie? Didn't Hamm call you when he got home? I bet he just got busy. I'm sure everything is fine."

I wiped my hand across my face and tried to ignore my growing sense of uneasiness. "You're right June. Thanks for keeping me sane. Let's go find out what this goon is up to before he hurts someone else."

We secured our purses cross-body, checked to make sure our shoes were tied, never mind I was wearing flip flops and

June's combat-style running shoes fastened with Velcro. We locked hands in a death grip usually reserved for midnight viewings of horror movies. When we were sure we were the only ones in the vicinity other than the squirrels, we snaked our way between the sparse saplings lining the edge of the woods. It wasn't long before we crept out from the trees and stood in the open in front of the building. The place was old. Where it was metal, it was corroded by rust, and the sections that were wood showed only a few shadows of its original, sunny-yellow paint. If the building was a person, it would be a zombie. The high windows around the structure's perimeter looked like empty eye sockets and prevented us, or anyone for that matter, from seeing inside.

June was jumping up and down under one of the windows. "We need to get inside. Those boxes must be important to somebody."

"Are you crazy? That's breaking and entering! What if we get caught? I don't want to spend my retirement years wearing an orange jumpsuit and showering with strangers."

"Who's going to catch us? It's not like there are nosy neighbors with binoculars keeping watch over the place, which is exactly why someone would choose it to hide illegal activities. If no one has stopped us by now, I think we're safe. Besides, if there happens to be a slightly open door or a broken window, we wouldn't technically be breaking, just entering."

I rolled my eyes at the back of June's head as she disappeared around the back of the building. "That makes me feel so much better."

I grudgingly decided I might as well follow her. We'd come this far and I did want to see what was inside the old building.

Maybe there was a service entry or some other way in. Circling the building, we came to a stop in front of a garage door in the back that was set sturdily and level in its frame, looking incongruous in the middle of the leaning, tired wall. It was obvious that care had been taken to add a secure entrance to the dilapidated structure. There was a gap under the door on the left side created by the unmatched angles just wide enough for a nosey snoop or two to shimmy through.

Before I could stop her, June was down on the ground doing a crab walk right under the door. When her entire body had disappeared into the creepy building, I was left standing on the outside, frozen in place. I didn't think this was a great idea. Seconds later, June's arm appeared under the door, jerking and gesturing wildly. I assumed she was telling me to follow her inside. So now I figured I had two options. I either continued standing out in the open, alone and scared half to death, or go inside and be scared half to death with June. I decided on the latter. Rather than contorting my body into the form of a crab as June had done, I got down on my hands and knees in front of the door. The gravel poked and scraped at my palms and exposed knees as I flattened myself and wriggled under the door.

Once inside the building, I straightened up, brushed the dust off my clothes, and picked some small stones out of my hands while I tried to get my bearings. The space was musty-smelling and damp. Dust mites danced and floated through the meager rays of sunlight filtering through the grimy windows. It was too dark to see much of anything, but I began imagining spiders, rats, and other creepy critters scavenging about. Instinctively, I rummaged in my purse for my phone.

How did people survive without phone apps in the frontier days? I used the flashlight app to shine a thin beam of light over the floor and up the walls. The interior of the warehouse was half the size of a football field. All around the room, boxes like the ones the mystery man had been delivering were stacked eight to ten high. The towers of boxes were covered haphazardly with ragged, dirty tarps. Along the wall to the left of the garage door stood a row of boxes that didn't have any others stacked on top. These must be the boxes we witnessed the man in black unloading from the van.

"This is crazy, June. We need to get out of here. Let's go call Detective Morgan so he can get a warrant or something and come check this out himself."

"There's no time. On an island this small, whoever owns this warehouse would catch wind of a warrant being issued and have plenty of time to clear out before the police ever got here. Besides, we don't even know what's in the boxes. We would have to tell Morgan what he was looking for before he could request a search warrant."

She had a point. It wasn't a crime to store boxes in a warehouse, even if you did look like a city-slicker career criminal. There was no turning back now. Like it or not, we were in this all the way. June walked toward the box closest to the door, and I approached one two spaces down. I worked at the shipping tape with the tip of my nail file and got the top opened without much problem. What I discovered in front of me was both exciting and disturbing.

Inside the box were designer handbags and scarves I could only dream about affording. I lifted out a beautiful, green leather tote with a chain-link handle and tried it on for fit over my arm. I only wished there was a mirror in the place so I could admire the chic way it hugged my figure. I imagined strolling down the street collecting compliments on my fabulous fashion sense. As I was on my third or fourth turn, I noticed the tag on the handle was not quite right. The metallic tone was a little too brassy. I stopped and took a closer look. The purse was indeed leather, but upon closer inspection, I noticed the materials were slightly less than designer quality. This was the best designer knock-off I had ever seen. It was impressive, and I'm sure most people would never know. I was not, however, most people when it came to knowing my accessories, especially handbags from my favorite designer.

June looked up from the box she was inspecting wearing a pair of Dolce & Gabbana sunglasses with large white plastic frames and black lenses. "These look killer with my outfit, don't you think?"

"June, these purses and scarves are all knock-offs."

"Huh? Are you sure?" She took the glasses off her face and carefully checked the hinges and markings inside the frames.

"Well I'll be darned. You're right. I didn't notice. They're excellent knock-offs, but they are most definitely fake. They're still cute, though, don't you think?"

Her box also contained silver necklaces and earrings I would have sworn belonged in little blue boxes, along with an assortment of other recognizable designer labels. I thought back to all the times I had admired some of these very accessories on the shelves of Ruby's Treasure Chest. My heart sank with the realization of what this meant.

"June, do you think Ruby knows about this? I can't imagine her ever trying to pass off fake merchandise as name brands."

"Well, somebody knows something. This stuff looks good, but someone was bound to notice eventually. I can't believe any of this has actually been on her shelves, can you?"

I didn't know what to think. "I suppose you could sneak a piece in with the real stuff here and there and fool a lot of people. But why? And look at all this stuff! If all these boxes are full of these things, where is it all going? More than one buyer would have to be involved to move all this merchandise."

Before we had time to speculate any further, June held up her hand in a sign to be quiet. "Sshh! Did you hear something? I thought I heard a car door."

"June, he's back," I whispered. We held our breath and listened to the squeak of the old door hinges at the front entrance. "Quick, let's get out of here!"

The entire space was suddenly flooded with blinding fluorescent light. I stood like a toddler with her hand in the cookie jar for what seemed like an hour, but more likely it was closer to five seconds. Then all bets were off. I dropped the fabulous green bag onto the dirty floor and ran like I was being chased by Satan himself toward the light shining under the garage door. I prayed June was behind me. I improvised a home run slide and rolled like an awkward burrito under the door until I lost momentum. Then I scrambled the rest of the way from the building back into the shelter of the thin tree line.

I watched as June followed my path and caught up to me seconds later. When I saw she was safe I remembered to breathe. We were stuck, crouched behind some thorny shrubs that may or may not have been poisonous. I heard music coming from close by. This must be it. The angels were playing their trumpets to usher me through the pearly gates. "Celebrate Good Times, Come On!"

Chapter Seventeen

It was my phone ringing. It must have fallen out of my pocketbook in the parking lot about three yards from where we were hiding. I didn't think about what I was doing as I sprinted out into the open to snatch it then scurry back to our hiding place. "Hamm! Hamm! Where are you? I need to talk to you! Something bad is going on. I know I promised, but we wanted to help and..."

"Please hold for the next available agent. Your call is important to us..."

"What? Who is this? What do you want?"

I didn't have time to figure out how the ringtone I had programmed for my husband was now heralding telemarketers. There were a lot of strange things happening, but I needed to focus on the most imminent danger—the stranger in the warehouse. It was time to take action.

I pressed the end call button with more force than necessary. "We can't take the bike. He'll see us for sure. We need another way to get back to the ferry without being spotted. There's a kayak rental place down by the shore and it's out of sight from the building and the place the goon's golf cart is parked. My chiropractor keeps telling me I should try kayaking as a physical activity. Maybe now's a good time to start."

"Really? Does he expect you to kayak three times a week all year? We live in Ohio, remember? Don't you think running or joining a gym might be a better option?"

"We don't have time to discuss the pros and cons of kayaking. Let's just go rent one and use it to get back to the ferry dock. We need to get back to the mainland. We should get to a safe place and tell the authorities what we've seen here. Hurry, June."

June didn't need to be told twice. She took off, her cute, army-boot-styled running shoes kept her sure on her feet as we sprinted across the sand. My fashionable flip-flops matched my outfit perfectly but were not holding up quite as well in the running department. June reached the brightly painted rental kiosk well before me and was stretching her hamstrings when I caught up with her, panting and trying to shake the sand out of my sandals. I approached the rental window, wallet in hand, ready to get on with our plan.

"Hello! Is anybody here? Hello! We need to rent a kayak!" There was no one to be seen anywhere near the rental station.

"Not again! Francie, you better pull a rabbit out of that magic bag of yours. And quick."

When it comes to improvising, I am nothing if not resourceful. I dug a page of a play script out of my bag and retrieved a tube of mauve lipstick that did nothing for my olive complexion. It was time to write another IOU, this time to the kayak rental company. Using my increasingly useful cell phone camera, I snapped a photo of June and myself holding the IOU and standing in front of the rental hut, friended the company on Facebook, and uploaded the picture to their business page. Under the picture, in the comment box, I typed the date and our names. At the last minute, I decided to add a smiley face icon in order to let the business owners know that we were friendly and trustworthy, not irresponsible jerks trying to take advantage of island hospitality. This was getting too easy.

Anxious to get far away from the stranger, we chose the kayak we felt was best for the job—the one with the pretty fish mural painted on the side. We each grabbed an end and ran down the beach toward the water. We were ankle-deep in the icy water and about thirty feet off shore when at last we were able to stop our forward momentum. June held the kayak steady as I hauled myself in. June hopped over the side and planted herself confidently behind me. We each detached an oar from the side clasps and got down to business.

About fifty yards from land, June tapped me on the shoulder. "Francie, are you okay?"

I wasn't rowing. I was staring at the open water. We weren't far from shore. Any sane person would have realized she could hop over the side and almost walk the whole distance back to the beach. It was no more than five feet deep in most places, so the worst that would happen might be the need to hop up and down a bit. I, however, had just realized our prettily painted vessel was not equipped with life preservers.

"Umm, June, remember that thing about me and not knowing how to swim? I do love the water, but I'm afraid I never got around to actually learning how to swim in it. Do you think this thing will make it to the ferry dock? I don't want to die, especially not in a kayak!"

"Don't worry," June said with a worried look on her face, not because she was afraid of meeting an untimely end, but because her friend was having a meltdown and she didn't have time to deal with it.

"This is a piece of cake, Francie. Don't think about it and start rowing."

The longer we oared, the harder it was getting for me to breathe. I knew I was being irrational, but I was also sure I was hyperventilating and didn't have anything stashed in my handbag to cure this particular condition.

"Why did I ever suggest getting in this deathtrap? And why did you agree to my hair-brained idea?"

"Well it seemed better than asking the creep in the warehouse for a ride back to town. Besides..."

The rest of June's comment was drowned out by the rumbling of a Jet Ski heading directly toward us. Just when I thought it would come barreling straight into our kayak, it turned sharply. Icy lake water sprayed high into the air and dropped onto us like frozen rain. June and I both grabbed the edges of the kayak and stared in disbelief as the maniac driver began circling us in a wild frenzy of waves and spraying water. As suddenly as the menacing watercraft had appeared, it took off, heading away from us and around to the other side of the island.

I gulped in my first full breath of air and was about to tell June that we were heading back to take our chances with the knock-off guy when the waves created by the watercraft's circling began to churn and collide with each other. We were being tossed this way and that, the nose dipping lower under water with each wave. I suddenly knew what it felt like to be an ice cube spinning in a blender of margaritas. The water was taking us along on a wild ride and more and more of the lake was making its way inside the kayak. The nose of our little vessel suddenly dipped so low into the water that I was thrust at least three feet above June's head. There was no longer the slightest question in my mind. We were going to get wet and I was going to die.

"Help me! Help me! I'm going to die!" In the blink of an eye, I was airborne and aiming for certain death at the bottom of the lake.

My hero, June, kicked it into high gear. Using her research and experience from one of her latest articles, "Women Who Lifeguard," for Hot Mammas magazine, she grabbed me a split second before I made contact with the water. Wrapping her right arm around my waist, she buoyed me up so we could both cling to the overturned kayak. "Hang on, Francie! Just hang on. We'll be fine."

"I am. I am! But I don't think I can do this much longer. I'm going to die!"

My hair was plastered to my neck and my eyes were burning from the eye makeup soup streaming down and around them. I had gulped down what felt like a quart of lake water and couldn't let go of the side of the boat to pick out a slimy strand of seaweed stuck in my teeth. Just when I thought it couldn't get any worse, it did. The thrumming of a small motor alerted us that a boat was approaching from behind. There was no way to turn around without letting go of the hull and ensuring certain death. I scrunched my eyes shut and held my breath. So this was it.

"I love you, Hammond. Why can't I ever just take your advice? I'm sorry Beth and Ben. I didn't mean to screw things up. Please don't hate me."

"What in God's name is going on here? What are you two doing floating around in the middle of the lake? Don't you know the water is barely forty-five degrees? You could get hypothermia if you're not wearing wet suits."

We of course were not wearing anything of the sort. I have never ever been so glad to have a handsome man see me looking like a refugee clown.

Detective Morgan hauled my water-logged, sobbing body over the side of his police motorboat while June hopped up and down in the icy water and tried to flip our borrowed kayak. Once I was seated and breathing reasonably, Morgan handed me an itchy wool blanket that, just then, felt like a cashmere robe wrapped around my shoulders. June launched herself over the side of Morgan's rescue vessel. She sat on the bottom, folded her arms around her knees, and managed to look cute and innocent. Maybe I need to get my hair cut.

Morgan gave us a moment to recuperate then simply said, "Spill it."

June went first since I was still wheezing. "Jack, thank you for rescuing us. Did you see the guy on the Jet Ski? He swamped us on purpose! We know who burned down Ruby's store, and we have evidence."

Morgan looked skeptical. I was starting to recover so I picked up the story. "There's something bigger than arson going on here. There's some sort of merchandise scam going on involving Roger and the guy who flipped us over. I'm sure he's not the brains of the operation though."

June interrupted. "I heard them talking behind the house. They said 'fire,' 'merchandise,' and 'money' for sure."

"Whoa. Back up. Who is 'them' and whose property were you trespassing on?"

"We weren't trespassing." We both chimed in.

June continued our story. "We went to console Ruby and offer to help in any way we could. She's our friend for crying out loud. We care about her."

I added, "I was speaking to Ruby, and June went around back to find Roger. She found him all right. He was whispering in the yard with the creepy mystery man. Then we saw him again at the warehouse, the creepy guy, not Roger. We saw him moving boxes of knock-off goods from his van to the warehouse. Then he tried to kill us!"

Morgan cut me off. "Enough. This is not some episode of CSI or a Nancy Drew novel." He stared at each of us in turn. "You two need to realize that you are interfering with a real-life police investigation. One in which, I might add, Hamm is a person of interest. Sometimes in real life there is no nice simple answer at the end of an episode as to why bad things happen or people get hurt."

He turned his back to us, took the wheel, and steered the boat back in the direction of the ferry dock, our defeated kayak trailing limply behind from a tow rope. For a few moments, the only sound was the steady rumble of the boat motor.

June couldn't take it and broke the silence. "We should go back. We can show you where the evidence is. You can find the bad guys and close this case."

The skipper kept his right hand on the wheel, never veering from his course.

"Ladies, I feel like I'm starting to sound like a broken record, but this is where your part in the investigation ends. I will take complete statements from both of you after you dry off and calm down. But then it ends. The police will do their job, and you will do nothing further to compromise this case. Do you understand?" His steely gaze made me feel like I was ten years old and being scolded by the principal for misbehaving (not like that ever happened).

June turned to Morgan, mollified, and said, "Yes, sir. We understand. We'll go home now and let you do your job. But please check into what we said. It's all true. I promise."

We were silent for the remainder of the short ride back to the island ferry dock. When Morgan pulled up, he left his motor running and looped a line casually around a cleat. I hauled myself over the side of the police boat and stood there awkwardly as the handsome detective put his hands on June's shoulders and said something to her that was inaudible to me. Their noses were practically touching. I assumed he was giving her one final warning to stay out of his way, but judging by the blush creeping across June's cheeks and the way Morgan gently tucked a few strands of wet hair behind her ear, it may have been something more personal. I had to admit, they looked good together. Moving apart while still keeping their gazes locked, he gave June a hand onto the dock.

Chapter Eighteen

We had about ten minutes to kill until the next ferry back to the mainland would arrive. Morgan gave us one last appraising stare. Then he turned to the gathering crowd and used his voice of authority. "Move along, people. There's nothing to see here."

The tourists waiting to board the ferry likely disagreed with the detective's statement. I was positive there would be a great deal of animated conversation about the two dripping crazy ladies on the ferry over cocktails tonight.

We purchased our return tickets with sopping money I managed to scrounge up from the bottom of my bag, which had miraculously stayed crossed over my shoulder during our stint in the lake. I looked at the soggy satchel and was thankful I had splurged on the purchase rather than buying a less expensive version of my bag. It had proven not only sturdy but also seaworthy. Huddling together in a thin sunbeam, we tried our best not to stand out like circus freaks who had been pushed into a dunking barrel.

Once we were on the ferry, we slumped on a bench near the back and tried to make ourselves as small as possible. I absently began pulling soaked newspaper shreds out of my purse trying to keep my mind from overloading on all of the trouble we had managed to get ourselves into.

"I think you're going to need a new copy of the paper for your article, June. It turns out The Tribune is not seaworthy."

"What do you mean? I'm not using anything from The Tribune for an article. The only thing I'm working on right now is this island thing that is turning out to be the exact opposite of the light piece it was supposed to be. Let me see that paper."

I handed June a piece that was less waterlogged than the rest. It contained the majority of an article and some evidence of red ink.

"That isn't mine. I just picked that paper up from where Michael left it so I could stay undercover at the market."

"Oh, I assumed you were the one who circled the article about a millionaire in Chicago who died in a fire. Maybe Michael knew him. Is he from Chicago? Wouldn't that be interesting?"

As if on cue, a dog began growling from the other side of the ferry. Michael and Gunner were standing at the rail and Sirena was walking past them. Go figure. It's always when you're out in public looking like a train wreck that you run into people you know, and it's usually the people you least want to see. I would love to ask Michael about the newspaper article, but I sure didn't feel like drawing attention to myself or initiating conversation in my soggy clothes and squishy shoes. I looked toward the pair, musing over the circled article and what, if anything, it might mean. Gunner was standing at attention. The fur stood up on his back, and he was growling at Sirena, who had stopped along the railing a little way past them. She must not be a dog person.

Another few moments ticked by, when the sound of a familiar voice enticed me to look up. Sirena, looking even lovelier than I remembered, was standing right in front of us. In her musical voice, she inquired, "What on earth happened to the two of you?"

For a moment, neither June nor I could find appropriate words to answer. June wore such a dejected look I was wondering if she was thinking that running into Sirena on the ferry from Kelleys to the mainland cemented the theory that she had spent the night with Cliff. The thought had crossed my mind. I wasn't sure why the idea bothered her so much though. It's not like she was interested in getting back with her ex.

June spoke first. "Sirena, something very sinister is going on around here, and I don't mean just the fire at Ruby's. We are positive it wasn't an accident, and we're pretty sure we know who started it."

Sirena looked startled. "How on earth could you know such a thing? The police don't have a clue."

"We tried to tell Detective Morgan what we discovered," June explained, "but he didn't want to listen to us. I heard Roger talking to a suspicious-looking man the day after the fire, and we sort of ran into the guy later on, and he sort of tried to kill us."

"What are you talking about?" Sirena was all ears now. She sat down on the bench across from us, looked from side to side, then leaned forward with her elbows on her knees and her hands clasped.

I took up the tale from there, adding specific details, while trying not to say anything too specific that might compromise the police investigation. "The unidentified man was selling knock-off products and passing them off as authentic to Ruby and Roger, and probably many others by the amount of evidence we discovered stashed in his hiding place, When Ruby discovered the deception, she must have threatened to expose him. Then he set fire to her store to destroy the evidence. Now he must be trying to get his merchandise off the island and cover up any paper trail that would lead back to him and incriminate him. We haven't yet figured out who he is or where he came from, and we have no idea who the poor soul who died in the blaze could have been. As far as we know, no one has been reported missing."

Sirena listened attentively, her sparkling green eyes fixed upon us in unwavering concentration. She changed the subject with a generous offer.

"Here, Francie, let me lend you this to keep you from getting hypothermia. You're still shivering." She offered me her dry sweater to replace my dripping one. The soft blue fabric matched the shade of my numb lips. I peeled my stretched-out cardigan off, dropped it in a puddle at my feet, and replaced it with Sirena's floaty, cover-up that still carried a faint scent of her amazing perfume.

"Thanks. That's very kind of you," I managed to reply through chattering teeth.

"Oh, don't worry about it. We'll catch up soon. Please keep me posted on your investigation, and let me know if there's anything I can do to help."

"Thank you. Keep your eyes peeled for anything suspicious and please be careful. There's a dangerous criminal somewhere nearby."

Sirena left us and walked completely around the deck, avoiding Michael and his dog. Stopping on the opposite side of the ferry cabin, she sat down by the window and looked out at the gray water of the lake. There was something ominous in the air. In spite of this, or maybe because of it, the rest of the short trip was blessedly uneventful, and no one else intruded on our shivering, sullen silence.

When the ferry stopped on the mainland, we hastened down the gangplank, across the parking lot, and back to my car.

Safely back in familiar surroundings, I let out a huge sigh of relief. Then I caught a glimpse of my reflection in the rear view mirror and gasped.

"Dear Lord! No wonder all those people were staring at us!" I turned to my right and took a closer look at my best friend on the seat beside me and burst into laughter—the kind that makes you gasp for air and grab your ribs.

"What are you laughing at? Are you in shock? Do you have brain damage?"

She stopped talking, took a good look at me and reached up and turned the rearview mirror toward her so she could inspect her own face. After that, it was all over. She started with a surprised giggle which turned into a chortle and then escalated into full-blown, cackling laughter.

June bent over in the passenger seat, trying to get her act together. She managed to catch her breath and say, "Let's get home. We're going to be arrested by the ugly police if we stick around here."

I got us back to the condo without incident. In the driveway, I turned to June and said, "Can you come in and maybe stay over? I'd like to talk about what happened and try to figure out what's going on."

"No problem. I wasn't looking forward to spending the night alone on my houseboat anyway. But maybe we should try to relax tonight. We can debrief in the morning. We could order a pizza."

"Pizza it is."

"With extra cheese!" We exclaimed in unison. Sometimes we scare me.

I pulled out my phone, which was in working order in spite of the ordeal in the lake. "I'll order it now, so we can take showers and change our clothes before it gets here. Some of Beth's clothes are in the guest room. I'm sure you'll find something that'll fit you."

We went inside and June made herself right at home. She had stayed overnight at the condo enough times that she referred to the guest room as her room. After a quick shower, she looked in the closet and opened several drawers, trying to decide on a comfy outfit. She chose one of Beth's tank-style tunics, and although they wear the same size, on June's slight frame, the pretty coral top reached just below her knees.

I showered too and changed into yoga pants and a well-worn, oversized knit shirt. This time comfort won over fashion, hands down.

I gathered up our wet, smelly clothes and was about to toss them in the washing machine when I spotted Sirena's sweater in the tangled mess. I picked it up, undecided whether to fold it or add it to the laundry pile. I didn't want to shrink it, so I turned it inside out and checked for the care label. "That was so nice of Sirena to loan me her sweater. I can't imagine what we looked like to her!"

"Hey, something just fell out of the pocket, Francie. You better not lose something of Sirena's after everything she's done for us!"

I read the tag that said "Dry Clean Only," then bent over to pick up the folded piece of stationery that had fallen from her pocket.

"This looks like some kind of a shopping list or a recipe, but it's not anything I'd want to eat."

"Let me see that." June took the slip of paper from my hand and read the list out loud: wax paper, dryer sheets, glycerin, triethylaluminum, eyelets, potassium permanganate, balloons.

"Seems fairly ordinary to me," I said, "except for the tri whatever and the pot of pomegranates. Just put it back in the pocket. It's probably stuff she needs for her shop, or a party, or something. She makes a lot of those fancy candles, soaps, and secret love potions from scratch I hear."

"I'm sure you're right. I hope she remembered to get everything on her list. Do you think we should call her and ask her if she needs it?"

"Oh, there's the doorbell. Dinner is served!"

We spent the rest of the afternoon and evening inside the condo devouring an entire cheese and mushroom pizza with extra cheese, sharing a bottle of California Red, and binge-watching the entire seventh season of Bones on Netflix, even though the weather had finally broken and it had turned into a glorious sunny day. At long last, we were stuffed and bleary-eyed—we had had enough of pizza and TV.

"I'm exhausted," I mumbled. "Let's get some sleep and figure all this out tomorrow. G'night!" I shuffled down the hall to my room and fell into bed.

THE NEXT MORNING, I woke up to the rich smell of the Starbucks Breakfast Blend I love so much. I followed my nose into the kitchen where I found June deep in thought, staring out the big picture window at the promise of a new day. The sun was just peeking up over the horizon. It was such a beautiful vista that for a second I forgot about the events of the previous day and stood there in my bare feet gazing out at the lawn and the lake beyond. Without wanting to break the mood with words, I headed for the refrigerator where I pulled out a dozen eggs, shredded cheddar, shredded mozzarella, an onion, fresh spinach, and mushrooms. Halfway through my omelet preparation, I went back to the fridge to retrieve a chunk of Swiss cheese. This was going to be another "extra cheese" kind of day.

June poured a second mug of coffee, added a splash of cream and two spoonfuls of sugar, and sat at the kitchen table while I finished preparing our breakfast.

"We need a plan, Francie," she said to my back. "We'll need more photos of the fake merchandise and the hiding place. Maybe we can find some more clues or evidence. We need to get some names or addresses so we can identify whoever is behind this operation. If we want Morgan to take us seriously and arrest the criminal, we're going to have to give the police something solid so they can get a conviction and make it stick."

I joined June at the table and placed a plate containing a perfectly executed cheesy omelet in front of her. "Yes. Then we can get Detective Morgan to clear up any suspicions about Hamm and prove the creepy stranger is to blame. I still haven't been able to reach Hamm. I'm starting to worry. I know he said he had a major case issue that came up, but he still should have checked in by now."

"I wouldn't worry. You know how he gets when he's eyeball deep in a tricky case. It's always right before you are about to call out the National Guard that he remembers to check his messages."

"I know you're right. I'm sure he'll call soon. He always does." I didn't sound convinced, not even to myself.

Chapter Nineteen

We lingered over our breakfast, discussing what we needed in order to carry out the plan beginning to take shape. As we finalized the last details, June popped out of her chair and exclaimed, "It's time to go. Grab your bag, Francie. I'll clear the dishes while you get ready."

June was eager to get started. I, as usual, had mixed feelings; I wanted to get to the bottom of this, but I had a bad feeling things were more complicated than we had imagined, and I didn't want me or any of my friends to get hurt trying to do a job we were not qualified to do and should leave to professional law enforcement. In the end, I left June to clean up the kitchen, got dressed, gathered up my things, and threw a few potentially useful items into my back-up leather satchel. At the last minute, I went back to my closet, and found my one pair of sensible shoes behind a bag of discarded items waiting to be donated. Something was telling me this was going to be a long day.

Our first stop was June's houseboat so she could freshen up and change into clean clothes that belonged to her. Walking toward the boat slip, I noticed June's "Ahoy Homies" dock mat was askew and caked in mud. "June?" I questioned.

She had noticed the same thing. "It wasn't me. I just put that mat out yesterday. It was fresh from the cleaner's bag."

Things were going downhill. We glanced about the area, looking for anything suspicious, and stepped onto the boat deck. The sliding door to the cabin was unlocked, but that wasn't necessarily alarming. Everyone was friends on the dock and looked out for one another. It was one of the few places left where it seemed unnecessary to lock your doors at night or while you were away. I reached down to pick up a folded newspaper from the deck.

"At least no one stole your USA Today. I know how you get when you don't get your news fix."

"Why do you keep assuming every newspaper you come across belongs to me? I get all my news online with my tablet. Let me see that. Maybe it's a clue."

June unfolded the paper and held it up in front of her face. I could clearly see her through the giant hole chewed through the middle of the page. "Those look like teeth marks. Who would chew on a newspaper and throw it onto your boat deck?"

"I think I have an idea. After meeting Michael and Gunner last summer, that dog seemed to take a shine to me. I kept finding dog biscuits and bones around my boat. I think it's Gunner's idea of a present for me. This year, he might think I would enjoy Michael's discarded newspapers. It's kind of sweet don't you think? Chances are it was the dog who got muddy footprints on my mat and turned it all around. You know, the simple, obvious explanation is usually the right one."

"If you say so. Let's check out the cabin. I need to wash the dog slobber off my hands."

June tossed the paper onto the deck chair and pulled the door open to peek inside. The drawers and shelves had clearly been rifled through, and the refrigerator was left open revealing that June's best bottle of Pinot Grigio was gone. It was obvious because it was the only thing she had stocked in the fridge so far.

"Well, that's just plain rude. They could have at least left a note."

"And I'm pretty sure the dog didn't snoop through your drawers and steal your wine."

After looking around the cabin systematically, June concluded that nothing was missing besides the wine. "We don't need to report this. Someone probably ran out of wine last night and decided it was better to borrow a bottle from me than to leave the compound and risk getting a DUI."

"By the looks of your dock mat, that was probably a wise decision. But, hey, what about your drawers?"

"Well, if they were looking for wine, they probably needed an opener too. I'm not too concerned. I'll probably get a call or a text this afternoon when the guilty parties are feeling better. This is nothing new. It's happened before, you know."

"I don't remember hearing about that," I said.

"Well, it wasn't a big deal. Last summer, while you and Hamm were at that drama convention in Las Vegas, I spent a few days up here by myself. I made sure my cupboard was stocked, unlike some people on the dock. After a long day at the beach, and dinner with my dock mates, I hung out with six or eight friends on the dock until around eleven. By then, I was worn out, so I went back to my boat and was sound asleep as soon as my head hit the pillow. At about two o'clock, I was sure

I heard someone walking around in the cabin. I stayed in my bed and didn't make a sound. Pretty soon I heard voices. I had my cell phone in my hand and 911 keyed in and ready to hit 'send.' After a minute of listening to whispering and giggling, I recognized the voices. Lucky for Jen and Mary Jo, I held off calling the cops."

I was standing in the galley, trying to put things back in order while listening to June continue her story from behind closed doors as she finished getting ready.

"Those are some friends, sneaking into your cabin in the middle of the night. They could have gotten themselves into a lot of trouble."

"Think about it, Francie. We'd have done the same thing under the circumstances. Jen just needed a free refill."

"I guess you have a point. Are you about ready?"

"Yes, I'm ready, but do you mind if I take a few more minutes before we head out? My curiosity has gotten the best of me, and I want to figure out what was in the gaping hole in the middle of the paper my buddy Gunner left me. It will just take me a second to pull it up online."

"Go for it, Madame Sherlock. I'd like to know what Scooby Doo is working on these days, too. You sure attract the good-looking ones, June!"

"I can't help it. Great minds and bodies think alike. Maybe one of these days, I'll find a stable man who will love me for the catch I am."

"Hey, here's your wine opener. It's in the drawer right where you always keep it. Either Jen didn't want to open your wine aboard your boat and risk spilling it, or she couldn't see what was right in front of her."

"It doesn't matter one way or the other. I only hope she enjoyed it, and next time I see her, I want to hear all about her evening of fun."

I finished tidying up the galley and left June to her research. When she reemerged, she was carrying several papers she had printed from her wireless printer, looking thoughtful, put-together and confident—the cool, professional journalist that she was.

"Well, what was the missing article about?"

"It was about a millionaire from Chicago who died."

I craned over June's shoulder to read the printed pages she was holding. "Was it in a fire? What's with all these Chicago stories? Do you think it's the same guy that was in the paper from the market?"

"I don't know, but I plan to find out. It says here his coin collection turned up in the possession of a New York mob boss. The mafia guy claims he took it as payment for a shipment of designer wholesale merchandise. The guy who paid with the coins is wanted for questioning and is suspected of having a partner. They are asking for leads to be directed to the FBI."

I straightened my shoulders, paced across the galley, and sat down heavily at the dinette. "Whoa! You don't think the guy from the warehouse could be the person they're looking for, do you?"

"I don't know. It doesn't seem like a big-time Chicago/New York criminal could possibly be operating from our little island." June shuffled through her papers again, scanning the contents for clues. "I guess it could happen, but let's check things out before we go to the authorities and end up getting ourselves an all-expenses paid stay in the looney bin."

"You're right. This makes getting to the bottom of all of the weird stuff going on around here seem even more important."

June folded the sheets of paper in half and tossed them on the end table. "I agree. I'm all set. Let's get going, and thanks for cleaning up the mess in here."

"No problem. It gave me something to do while you got ready."

June made sure to lock the door behind her this time. "It was nice of Lynn to loan you her jet boat for the day. Having our own transportation will make things a whole lot easier, and speaking of transportation, we need to remember to settle up with the bike and kayak rental places while we're over there."

I fished in my bag, pulled out two envelopes, and waved them toward June. "I'm a step ahead of you on that one. I figured out what we owed each place and put money in envelopes with their names on them."

"How much do I owe you? I'll pay half."

I tucked the envelopes back into my bag. "I'm not worried. I know where you live. I'm guessing the kayak is at the police station. I hope they're not planning to keep it as part of the investigation. We'll need to get it back so we're not charged for an extra day's rental."

"Investigation? Of what, Francie? Morgan probably can't stop laughing every time he thinks of the two of us hanging on to that thing for dear life. I don't think he took us too seriously. That's why we need to go back to the warehouse and get some real evidence."

"What about the bike, then? We left it in the trees by the warehouse. We need to get our act together and quit leaving borrowed means of transportation all over the place before we end up getting arrested like those minnow bandits. Instead of solving this mystery, we might find ourselves being charged with stealing and who knows what else."

"Well, if the man in black hasn't found it yet, it might actually come in handy later. We'll be able to ride it back into town and return it in person after we finish what we need to do."

"Let's go get the boat and get this show on the road."

"Amen to that."

My friend Lynn and her husband, Greg, have a summer place right next to ours. She never takes her jet boat out on the lake until the water has warmed up enough to swim in, which usually means the end of June at the earliest, so when I called her to ask if I could borrow it for the day for an excursion over to Kelleys Island, she never hesitated. She left the ignition keys under her front door mat. They were now in my hand and we were ready to get under way. Piloting a small jet-engine boat was something I had a lot of experience doing; Hamm and I had spent many long afternoons on the bay, tubing and water skiing with the twins over the years, and I knew Lynn kept coast guard-approved personal flotation devices on board. This time, I was prepared.

I was feeling confident for the first time in several days as we set out on foot to cover the quarter mile distance to the jet boat dock. I was also feeling proud of myself for getting in some extra exercise to compensate for the cheese splurges we'd been indulging in recently.

"June, could you slow down please?" I needed a few minutes to ease into this activity.

As usual, June was eager to get to our destination and had me trying to keep pace with her brisk walk, which could almost certainly be considered a jog. I'll be sure to record it as a jog in my Weight Watchers tracking journal; every little bit helps.

"Hey, Francie, there's a note here on the windshield. It's probably from Lynn." June had reached the boat before me, and she was neither breathing heavily nor perspiring. I was doing both. She handed me the folded paper and waited for me while I dug my reading glasses out of their special inside pocket in my bag and read the note.

Stay away from the island and mind your own business. You never know what kind of accidents can occur out on the water.

"What does it say, Francie? Did Lynn leave us any special instructions? Does she want us to pick something up for her?"

"Not exactly. It isn't signed but it's from someone who says we need to stay away from the island. How could anyone know we were going to take Lynn's jet boat over to Kelleys? Someone is watching us, June. This is not good. What do you think we should do?"

"We need to do exactly what we planned. We need to get back into that warehouse and get the evidence we need to convince Jack to take us seriously. It's the only thing that will identify whoever is behind this trouble and get Hamm's name off the list of persons of interest."

"Okay, I agree we need to help this investigation along. The police seem to be looking in all the wrong places."

When we got aboard the boat, the first thing I did was check the compartment where the life jackets were stowed. They were all there. Then, I took June's camera bag and placed it with my purse and the tote bag holding the supplies we would need to put our plan into action next to the PFDs and closed the hatch. We were ready to embark on our day's mission.

I turned the key in the ignition and smiled as the engine sprung to life. "Put your shades on and sit back for a lovely cruise, June. I'll have you on the island in no time."

Chapter Twenty

The water was smooth and the air was warm as we prepared to make our way across the lake for the fifth time in two days. The fun seekers planning to spend the day on water skis, Jet Skis, and boats of all sizes had not yet rolled out of their beds to begin their afternoon fun in the sun.

"June, keep your eyes open for any sinister watercraft. I sure as heck don't want a repeat of yesterday's debacle."

"Aye, aye, Skipper! I'm on it."

As we left the channel, I scanned the water, keeping a close eye out for any demented villain speeding into our path from the other side of the breakwall, and June watched the waters behind us in case someone approached from behind.

We hadn't gotten to the open water at the end of the No Wake Zone when June tapped my shoulder and pointed toward the beach near the end of the break wall. I couldn't hear her over the sound of the engine, but I saw she was motioning for me to slow down. The spot on the beach she was indicating was the same spot I had found her the night before with Michael and Gunner.

I put the jet boat in neutral so I could hear what June was saying.

"What is it, June? Is everything okay?"

"I don't know, Francie. I think I see Gunner pacing over there on the beach. I don't see Michael anywhere though. He never leaves Gunner by himself. This seems wrong."

Well, at least it wasn't someone trying to kill us, but I could tell June was worried, and I trusted her intuition as much as my own.

"I'll pull up as close to the beach as I can. Maybe we'll be able to see Michael if we get closer.

I angled the boat so we could get as close to the breakwall and shore as possible and idled in as close to the rocks as I dared. We could see Michael's dog pacing back and forth on a small stretch of beach. On the breakwall behind him, a form was sprawled on the rocks.

"Do you see that, Francie? Do you see the rocks behind Gunner? I think it's Michael."

"Oh my gosh, you're right! Do you think he fell?"

"Quick, pull the boat onto shore. We have to help him."

"Okay. I'm trying to get as close as I can without grounding it. There's an anchor in the compartment next to the one with the life jackets. We're going to have to jump out and anchor it offshore. Then we should be able to walk right up to the spot and see what's going on."

Once again June and I found ourselves in the freezing water of Lake Erie. At least this time, the water level stopped below our knees, and I was not in fear of drowning. By the time I got the anchor set, June was climbing up the slippery limestone rocks at the edge of the beach. Gunner was right beside her, navigating the jagged rocks like a pro, heading toward the form we had seen from the boat. I grabbed my phone from my bag and walked to the place on the beach where flat land met slippery stone. I stayed on the beach because climbing boulders in my flip flops would likely result in a trip to the emergency room for me along with Michael, or whomever it was, who was sprawled on the rocks.

"Hurry, Francie, it is Michael. He's unconscious. I think he fell and hit his head. There's a lot of blood. Call 911."

I punched in the emergency number and gave our location and a quick description of the crisis to the dispatcher. The calm voice on the other end informed me that police and an ambulance would be on their way and instructed me to stay on the line. We were to put pressure on any bleeding and not move the unconscious person. I relayed the information to June who was one step ahead. A familiar-looking green army jacket was folded up under Michael's head and she was using a sleeve torn from his tee shirt to put pressure on the cut above his eye.

"Is he breathing?"

"Yes. He's breathing, but it looks like he's been out here for a while. I don't want to climb down and leave him, so I'm going to throw Gunner's leash and Michael's backpack down to you. I wouldn't want the poor guy to get nervous and run off when he hears the sirens."

A sturdy leather leash and a worn leather backpack landed at my feet. I could hear sirens getting closer. Picking up the pack, I walked toward Gunner with his leash in my outstretched hand.

"Come here, boy. It's going to be okay." I squatted in front of Gunner and held out my hand so he could sniff me and assess my friendliness factor. He approached warily, took stock of my demeanor, and deciding I meant him no harm, stood beside Michael's backpack at attention. I gave him a minute to adjust to my presence then clipped the leash to his collar. He looked up at me with his soulful brown eyes, lay down in the sand, and rested his head on the familiar backpack. There wasn't anything else I could do at the moment, so I sat down in the sand beside him and stroked his velvety ears. We watched together as two men in white polo shirts and white pants briskly walked toward us with a stretcher and other assorted medical gear. A female officer followed close behind. She stopped for a moment to get my name, then climbed the rocks up to Michael and June. I craned my neck upward to see her writing in her notebook as she alternately asked questions of the medical personnel and spoke to June.

In less than fifteen minutes, the rescue and police vehicles were on their way, lights flashing and sirens screaming. When they were gone, June made her way down from the rocks and sat beside Gunner and me.

"What did they say, June? Is Michael going to be okay? Could they tell what happened? Was it an accident?" I was overflowing with questions, but there weren't many satisfying answers.

"The medics said the only injury was a laceration on Michael's forehead, but he was still unconscious and had lost quite a bit of blood. They are going to do some tests and stitch up the cut, but the rest depends on him waking up. The police have my phone number. They'll call me when he regains consciousness. They have some questions for Michael when he wakes up. They did say that based on the type of injury, they couldn't say conclusively whether or not it was an accident. It may have been intentional, and that changes everything."

"What do we do now? We have to find somewhere for Gunner until Michael is better. We can't bring him with us to Kelleys. That is, if you still think we should go."

"Well, we can't do anything else for either of them sitting on this beach. I feel like Michael's accident is related to everything else that's been going on. Let's have a look in his backpack. Maybe we can find an address or phone number of someone who could watch Gunner."

A low growl came from Gunner's throat as June reached for the backpack under his head. She looked him in the face and never broke eye contact as she gently tugged the pack away from the loyal dog's protective custody. When she had moved it a safe distance, she sat back down, petting him and making soft, reassuring cooing sounds close to his ear. Gunner relaxed and lay down in the sand. I watched with interest as June opened the backpack and systematically began retrieving items: several newspapers, a notebook, a crumpled candy wrapper, dog biscuits, a sweatshirt, a Swiss army knife, a flashlight, and a gun.

"Oh my god, June, that's a gun!" She was holding the weapon by the barrel with her hand stretched out away from her.

"I know. Don't touch it. I don't know how to tell if it's loaded or not. Here, take this notebook and the newspapers, and I'll stash the rest of this stuff back in the bag. The last thing we need is for someone to see us out here with a misplaced dog and a gun."

"If I didn't know better, I would think we were magnets for disaster."

"I know, Francie, but if we can do anything to help, we have to at least try. Give me those newspapers and you look through the notebook. Hopefully something will give us a clue."

I scanned Michael's notebook, feeling guilty for looking into the personal thoughts of a man who clearly valued his privacy. The majority of entries were dates and times with some names of people and what I assumed were businesses. There were also some scientific or medical-sounding words with definitions and various notes. It mostly read like a timeline beginning the previous spring. The last entry was from last night. I noticed the name Overmayer about halfway down the page. For some reason that seemed to stick in my mind. "I can't decipher all these names and dates. It seems like Michael was tracking something or someone, but there isn't any indication about what it all means. And I don't think there is anyone in here he would want us to leave his dog with." I fingered the discarded candy wrapper as I mulled things over. It smelled vaguely like chocolate.

"I'm not getting anywhere with these newspapers either. They all pertain to that guy who died in Chicago and a missing coin collection. There are some from The New York Times about a mob connection to a ring of knock-off wholesale distributors. None of it seems to go together. I wonder why Michael is so interested in this guy."

I lay my hand on Gunner's neck and he gave me a thank you lick on the knee. "Well, where does that leave this furry guy?"

"I suppose we could bring him back to your condo. I mean, he was in the Army. I'm sure he wouldn't cause too much trouble."

"I guess so. He'll probably be better behaved than the twins were when they were younger and running wild around the place."

"That's true. Let's see if Gunner will get into the jet boat. I know he rides on the ferry, so hopefully he likes the water as well."

June waded into the cold water and hopped in the boat. Gunner tilted his head questioningly as he watched her.

"Here, boy!" With one whistle from June, Gunner was bounding through the water and flying over the side of the small boat which tilted precariously while Gunner shook his fur with vigor, drying off his coat.

Gunner was a great first mate. "I'm pretty sure he's done this before. He almost looks like he's smiling."

June grinned as she watched the expression of sheer joy on the dog's face. "Maybe I should get a dog. He seems so content."

"Maybe you should act like a dog. Try opening your mouth and sticking your face full into the wind."

It felt good to laugh for once and live in a happy moment, even if that moment would not last long.

When we got back to the condo, I pulled the jet boat up to the beach in my backyard. It seemed pointless to tie it up in the slip, just to turn around and undo it all in a few minutes. It was nice to step out of the boat onto warm sand instead of flash-freezing our feet in the lake water. Gunner followed June and seemed relaxed as he investigated the yard and the deck. Once inside he made himself comfortable on the kitchen floor.

"Let's give him a bowl of water and get back to our plan. We need to get to the warehouse before it gets too late."

"Sounds good. I think he'll be fine here for a couple of hours. I hope we hear from Michael soon. He'll be worried sick about his best friend when he wakes up."

"As soon as we get back, we'll call the hospital to check on him. They should have all of his test results by then."

"Time to try this adventure again. Do you have everything? Adhesive remover? Skin cleanser? Comb?"

"Really, June? You're talking to the master here." Hang on one second. I might as well return Sirena's sweater to her after we finish up. I'll grab it real quick."

The sweater was folded on top of the freshly laundered clothes we were wearing yesterday during our "swim" in the lake. Brrrr. I didn't want to think about that. It might be August before I feel like going for a dip in the lake this year. I checked to make sure Sirena's shopping list was still in the pocket, then headed back to the kitchen.

"I'm all set. We'll see you in a little while, Gunner. Be good." I bent down to pet the lounging dog. He growled and the hair on the back of his neck stood straight up. "What's wrong, Gunner? Calm down boy." He continued to growl at me and began barking and backing me into a corner of the kitchen. "June, do something! What's gotten into him?"

"I don't know. Throw me that sweater so you have your hands free in case he jumps up. I'll look for some cheese or something to distract him."

"Good idea. Catch!"

I flung the delicate sweater toward June and it floated toward the snarling dog and onto the floor between us. Gunner pounced on it and began tearing and ripping it to shreds. "Oh my gosh, June. Gunner ruined Sirena's sweater. She's going to kill me."

"It looks like the sweater is what made him so aggressive to begin with. Now that it's destroyed, he's sleeping like a baby."

"Remember how he was growling at Sirena on the ferry? She must not be a dog person. I think they can sense that sort of thing. I picture her with a cat."

"Maybe it wasn't her. Maybe it was the sweater. There could have been some scent or something in the fabric that irritated him. Dogs have very sensitive noses, you know."

"That sweater did smell good," I recalled. "Well, hopefully she's a people person and will forgive me when I tell her about the sweater. Let's head out."

"See ya, Gunner!" June gave him a pat on the head as we left the kitchen. He didn't even twitch an eye.

Chapter Twenty-One

About ten minutes later, we arrived at our destination, half the time it took us on the ferry. I pulled the jet boat up to Cozy Cove, a small marina located about a half mile west of the more popular tourist docking locations. This one was mainly used by locals who didn't care to be in the middle of the summer vacationers' round-the-clock revelry.

It was time to execute part one of our crime-solving game plan. After paying the real-live dockmaster with genuine currency, which reminded me that we needed to repay yesterday's IOUs, we headed straight to the small bathhouse reserved for marina guests.

Once inside, I plopped the tote bag and my purse on the counter and we got straight to work. I felt the same adrenaline rush as the backstage preparation right before a show. Getting into character always filled me with excited anticipation, and this wasn't simply a stage performance; it might be the biggest role I would ever be cast in.

"Come on, Francie, it's now or never. Pass me the adhesive and let me know when my mustache is straight."

"I will, but give me a second. My hair is fighting this hat with everything it's got."

I continued stuffing rogue curls under an unremarkable tan canvas hat as June wiggled a fake mustache up and down above her lip until it was as straight as it was going to get.

"So, do we look like the Fresh Market delivery guys or what, Francie? I can hardly recognize myself."

I scrutinized our disguised reflections in the mirror and had to admit, we might get back to the warehouse undetected. "I guess we won't know until we try. It's show time!"

"Here's to us. Let's go break a leg!"

"Or not. I never did like that expression. We can do this!"

We high-fived each other, took one last appraising look at ourselves, gathered up our props and headed for the door.

Cautiously at first, we emerged from the bathhouse. I peered around the corner of the door and scanned the area. "The coast is clear." Thankfully, there was no one in the vicinity to question what two Fresh Market delivery men were doing in the women's restroom. After that, it was a breeze. Not a single person looked twice at our nondescript uniforms as we made our way out of the park and on to the main street.

"It must be close to lunchtime," June remarked, pulling her phone from the pocket of her dark blue work trousers to check the time. "We better refuel before we get started, don't you think? We have to keep our energy up for the task ahead."

I couldn't disagree. The Sand Bar, a small, family-owned establishment, was a short way up the road from Cozy Cove and was popular with the permanent residents for their ice cold draft beer, fresh perch, and fabulous grilled-cheese sandwiches. We headed straight for the outdoor bar. I hesitated for a moment when I realized the bartender on duty was one I had seen before. In fact, the last time I was here with Hamm for lunch, he got irritated with the guy for flirting with me. He told me my smile could chase away any rain cloud and was offering me free drinks until my husband asked him about the current status of his liquor license.

Here was our chance to test our disguises. I placed my order for a grilled cheese sandwich and a Corona Light with a serious expression on my face, hoping my curls would remain under my cap. June settled on queso cheese dip with chips and a regular Corona. Our orders were delivered quickly and the bartender never gave me a second glance. I was a little disappointed that my sunny smile wasn't about to rate me a free drink today, but then I mentally slapped myself for even thinking such a thing. This was no time for flirtations. I should be joyful that my talents for dramatic costuming had gotten us past this first test of theatrical subterfuge.

We weren't even finished congratulating ourselves on our excellent acting skills when June shifted her gaze downward and lowered her voice to a near whisper. "Don't look now, Francie, but this could be bad, very bad. Detective Morgan is right over there and he's looking this way."

"How is it that this guy shows up everywhere we go?" I used all my resolve to keep my expression neutral and my head turned away. My uniform hat was doing a nice job of completely covering my unruly curls.

Our disguises must have been effective because although his eyes were squinting in our direction, he did not approach. Also to our advantage, our faces were shaded by the bar's canopy; so we ate our lunches and drank our beers quickly, then left the bar through the side exit with our backs to the pesky law man.

"I can't help but worry about finding Michael unconscious on the beach. Do you think we should have told Morgan about what happened? I'm sure he's going to find out. I don't want it to look like we're hiding things from him."

"The medics took down all our information. We weren't trying to conceal anything, at least not from them. I think it's best not to get involved for right now. Besides, we're delivery men. What would we know about it?"

"Good point. I almost forgot."

Hopefully Morgan didn't recognize the seductive sway of June's hips that even the baggy work pants couldn't conceal. He left at the same time, but headed in the opposite direction toward the street. We had passed test number two.

I ventured a quick glance behind me. "Our disguises are obviously working, but we better start being more observant. We should have seen his car parked right out front. That was too close for comfort."

"You are absolutely right, Francie. Let's get going, and let's keep our eyes and ears open from now on."

We walked along, following the path worn through the trees by the tires of many golf carts heading toward the lake. The abandoned warehouse was not in sight, but we knew it was close. While we walked toward our destination, we went over the details of our plan one more time.

After making a careful circle of the building, we concluded the van was not on the premises and the golf cart was still tucked away from view under its tarp. It was now or never.

The heavy garage door at the back of the warehouse was still securely locked, so once again we squirmed our way through the gaps in the siding and under the door. With all the added security to the old place, one would think the masterminds of this operation would have thought to repair the obvious problem. Oh well, it worked for us.

Near the front office of the dilapidated building, June located the switch for the overhead lights. They came on slowly and with the whiny sound of fluorescent bulbs not long for this world. The inside of the building lit up, but I could now see the flickering bulbs were dangling precariously from the loft's ceiling beams. Wild shadows danced eerily over the walls and floor of the drafty building like ghouls at a monster mash.

"This place is starting to creep me out, June. If it wasn't for poor Ruby and Roger, and the fact that my husband is being implicated in all this, I'd be out of here before you could say chocolate martini."

June was unpacking her fancy camera equipment she uses on assignment, so I took a nice, deep yoga breath to calm myself and walked over to the far wall to take a closer look at more of the stacked boxes.

I split the packing tape on the top of the first large cardboard box I reached with the hot pink mini box-cutter I had added to my bag this morning. The first thing I pulled out was a pair of royal blue patent leather sandals just like the ones I tried on at Macy's last week. They were even my size.

"These are amazing reproductions," I whispered toward June's general location.

I was amazed and impressed, and frankly overwhelmed, as I opened box after box uncovering more and more knock-offs of high-end brands favored by many stylish ladies. Coach and Gucci handbags in one box. Balenciaga scarves and Yves St.

Laurent sunglasses in another. The luxury items were too numerous to name or count.

I looked up from the growing mountain of goods to see June studying what looked like packing lists attached to a clipboard that hung on the wall.

"Come here, Francie," she called to me. "This doesn't look good."

She reached for her camera and focused the high-power zoom lens on the names and addresses of several boutiques located on the island and a few more on the mainland. When I got close enough to read the smaller tickets, I saw receipt after receipt all signed by Roger Burns. By the looks of it, Ruby's Treasure Chest was a regular buyer of the beautiful contraband.

"Where is all of this stuff coming from? There must be a company name on one of those receipts or packing lists."

June continued flipping through the stack of paper slips. "Wait. I found something."

I craned my neck to read the small print without the aid of my reading glasses. The poor lighting wasn't making it any easier. "What? What does it say? I give up."

"This one says 'Overmayer Overnighter.' I bet it's the name of some sort of transport business. I can look online to see if it's legitimate. Maybe we can backtrack and trace the source of these boxes through their travel history."

"Overmayer. Hmmm. Why does that name sound familiar? Where have I heard it?"

"Well, gee, Francie, that narrows it down."

"There's no need to get sarcastic. Don't worry. It'll pop into my head when I least expect it."

"Well, let's hope it's before your seventieth birthday."

"Never mind. We need to keep searching for clues and figure out what's going on." The tension in the room was palpable. We got back to work.

June snapped photos of all the written evidence before turning her attention to the boxes and the goods strewn about the floor. I decided to walk the perimeter of the building and look for more clues. I didn't know what I was looking for, but I was sure I'd know it when I found it. I passed rows and rows of boxes, picked up a ball of fluff that thankfully didn't turn out to be a mouse, and tripped on the bottom step of a rickety staircase. I had made it almost around and back to June but so far had come up empty-handed (except for the fluff). She was just raising her eyes from her camera when the room was plunged into total darkness.

"What the...?" I whipped my head around trying to see something. Anything. "June, are you okay? Where are you?"

"I'm here, Francie. Right here."

We shuffled our feet and stretched out our arms in the direction of each other's voices until our fingertips touched. Our fingers locked, and we threw our bodies at one another. We froze in place and waited for our eyes to adjust to the inky darkness. When that happened it was easier to assess our situation.

"I'm surprised those lights stayed on as long as they did," June whispered. "They didn't look too stable from the get-go."

"I know." I replied. "We need to make our way back to those boxes I was looking in when we first got here. My phone is still over there. We can use our flashlight apps to get out of here without getting hurt."

"My phone's in the front pocket of my camera case. It's so dark I can't see it from here. Hopefully, I'll be able to grab it on our way to get yours."

We shuffled and groped our way back to the spot where the boxes of knock-offs were strewn about. I dropped down on my hands and knees, and June bent over the disarray to help me locate my missing phone.

I was still rummaging through all the stuff when June stood up with my phone in her hand. I was about to hug her when she let out a yell that pierced my eardrums like a poisoned syringe.

"Francie, quick! We need to get out of here."

The next breath I took told me the whole story. The place was filling up with acrid smoke. I grabbed June's hand and she pulled me to my feet.

We found the exit door without a problem. It didn't take long to realize; however, that it was locked tight from the outside, and no amount of pulling, pushing, or banging would budge it. We couldn't make it to the gap under the garage door entrance either. It was across the room and there was thick black smoke and flaming boxes and merchandise blocking our path.

"Up there! The windows. We need to get to the windows!"

I knew it was the only other means of escape. But we needed to get there. The windows were nearly at the roofline, and the stairs I had tripped over minutes ago were probably as deadly as the smoke. We determined they were intended to lead up to some additional storage under the rafters, and we also surmised that they wouldn't support a forty-pound child, let alone two grown women. We had no other choice. It looked like we were going to have to take our chances.

June grabbed my arm. "We need to move fast. Find something we can use to break the window. I'll look for something to break our fall."

I remembered hearing June talk about the work she'd done on an article for Sexy Men in Suspenders last winter. She had explained to me that in a burning building, oxygen doesn't last long, especially the higher up in the room a person was. We needed to work fast. I searched for something we could use to smash those windows. They were single panes of glass, so it shouldn't be too hard. "Here's an umbrella I think will do the job."

"Okay. Good. Now we need something to break our fall so we don't break our legs. Oh no! I jinxed us when I said that stupid stage phrase I thought was good luck."

"Snap out of it, June. We don't have time for you to panic right now." I couldn't remember ever seeing her so close to losing control. She was supposed to be the calming presence in our duo.

"Okay, wait, I think I might have an idea." She rubbed her fists in her eyes, ran her fingers through her hair, and shook her hands vigorously at her sides. "Do you still have those water-activated rafts you bought at Sirena's shop?"

I rummaged in my handbag and found the turquoise iridescent shopping bag containing the novelty rafts. "Yes, here they are. I have them both."

My smile of accomplishment faded the instant I realized what was missing. "How are we going to activate this thing?"

June was one step ahead ransacking boxes in search of some kind of liquid. By sheer luck, she stumbled upon three cases of Veen, argued to be the freshest and purest water in the world.

Good thing it was fake. At forty dollars a bottle for the real stuff, we would have had to think twice about what we were about to do with it.

The air was getting thicker with smoke. "Use these," I gasped and tossed June some stylish Hermes scarves to cover our faces.

We breathed through the scarves and clutched as many bottles of water as we could, stumbling our way to the perilous staircase leading to the upper level of the warehouse. By this time, flames were licking the edges of the doors and smoke was taking the place of oxygen in our lungs. On the third step, I heard a crack beneath me, and my foot went right through the plank. A splinter the size of a sequoia tree ripped into my shin, but I didn't have time to stop. I had to get to the top before the whole thing collapsed under me.

Finally, I made it, gasping and choking, to a narrow walkway beneath the windows looking out over the wooded lot behind the structure. Once I got my balance, I clutched my fancy counterfeit umbrella baseball bat-style and whacked at the glass like I was in the ninth inning of the deciding game of the World Series.

Meanwhile, June uncapped water bottles with a vengeance and poured their contents over a raft that was meant to be a gift for one of my children.

"I may never see my sweet babies again. We've gotta get out of here!"

As soon as the water hit the raft, it began to enlarge and bloat up like a giant pillow.

"Hurry Francie. Clear the jagged glass from the window edges so we don't puncture this thing! It's almost too big to fit out the window as it is."

"It's all clear. Hurry June, hurry!"

There was barely enough time and space for June to dump the last bottle of water onto the raft and shove it out the window. It landed on the debris-covered ground twenty feet below us with a strange, slurpy thud.

"On the count of three. One. Two..."

"Wait. Do you mean *on* three or *after* three?" It seemed important to me at the moment.

June tugged me to my senses and we jumped as if our lives depended on it. (Oh yeah, they did.)

We landed in the middle of the enormous, spongy raft; elbows and knees flailing and bumping until we came to rest in a tangled heap. "Are you okay, June?"

"I think all my body parts are intact. My camera, not so much."

We struggled to free ourselves from the flotation device and stepped back to take a look at the damages.

"Oh my God! What is that thing? June, what is that?"

June was beside me, speechless for the first time I can remember. When she recovered enough to form words, she sucked in air and tried to reply. I wasn't sure if she was gasping, crying, or laughing. I was still staring in disbelief.

"It's a... It's a... Oh my gosh! It's a giant penis!"

"So, I wasn't hallucinating from the smoke."

"Francie, what did you buy? Wasn't that supposed to be for the twins? What's wrong with you?"

Of course, I had no idea what shapes the dehydrated rafts would become when water was added to the last-minute gifts. I didn't read the fine print on the package. My reading glasses were always in my voluminous purse, but not always accessible when I forgot to stash them in their designated pocket.

"Geesh. I'm wearing my glasses from now on. At least in the checkout aisle. Thank goodness that thing never made it to its intended destination."

Not a full minute had passed when Detective Jack Morgan came roaring up the street, lights flashing and sirens blaring, and screeched to a halt in front of us. He got out of the car slowly, put his hands on his hips, and stood staring at us with those soul-piercing eyes, mentally taking inventory of the scene before him, right down to the sticks and soot clinging to our no-nonsense tan and navy blue work uniforms. What could we do except stand there slumped, defeated, and in my case, bleeding, in front of the giant pornographic floaty toy. I'm sure the corner of his lip was twitching. To his credit, he neither laughed nor yelled at us.

Chapter Twenty-Two

June broke out of her mortified silence before I did, and went from zero to one hundred in a matter of seconds. She hurled herself at the detective and began babbling about how he was our hero and how scared we were. After that, it became hard to hear what she was saying due to the wailing of the four volunteer fire trucks that had arrived seconds behind Morgan.

"Thank goodness you showed up. Now you can arrest the person trying to ruin Ruby's life. And murder us."

"I don't think I'll actually murder you, but you two certainly are causing a lot of commotion around here."

"Huh? You know what I meant. Someone is trying to kill us."

Morgan held June for a moment and let his gaze take in her sweet, pixie-like features streaked with ashy soot and complemented by a crooked dangling mustache. He composed himself and set her aside, but his eyes held her for an extra beat.

Meanwhile, I overheard the volunteer firefighters who were not having any luck curtailing the inferno. They had decided to let it burn out as a controlled fire and concentrated on keeping it from spreading to the trees and vegetation around the building. What I gathered from their conversation was that the abandoned structure's value was minimal compared to the risk of harm to the men on the job.

"Listen to me!" I cried, as I ran back and forth between Morgan and the fire chief. "All the evidence will be destroyed. We have to get back in there. We have to prove what was going on. These knock-offs might be linked to the mob and some rich dead guy from Chicago."

Morgan stood his ground. "Listen, ladies. There's a lot more to worry about than some fashion crime. A murder victim was found in the debris at Ruby's, and so far, the only suspects of any crime happen to be the two of you and your husband, Francie. And by the way, where is Mr. Egge? He still isn't returning my calls to either his cell phone or the messages I left with his office."

I responded automatically. "He left for home yesterday morning. Something came up at work that needed his attention."

June's eyes were wide with shock. "Murder victim? What are you talking about? Who is it? What happened? You mean it wasn't an accident?"

I was one step behind in my reaction to what Morgan had just said. Thinking about Hamm had sent my attention in another direction.

"Wait a minute. Start over. I know that you said that someone died in the fire at Ruby's. Are you saying now that it was intentional?"

Now Morgan was looking concerned. How did everything go so terribly wrong in such a short time?

When Detective Morgan spoke next, he directed his words at me. His voice was low and controlled.

"Francie, no one from Hammond's firm has had any contact with him since Thursday afternoon. Are you saying you haven't heard from him, either? He is currently wanted for questioning, so if you know something, you better tell me right now. This is serious. I'm sure by now you are aware of the incriminating remarks your husband made to Mrs. Burns. Numerous people from the Beacon Pointe Yacht Club have also corroborated his threatening remarks. Apparently, it's no great secret how Hammond felt about the Burns' establishment.

"Listen Francie, I hate to be so hard on you, and I'm trying my best to get the facts straight because, frankly, after spending some time with him, I didn't think he was the kind of guy who could pull off such a thing. I'm a pretty good judge of character, but I have to say that right now things are not looking good for your husband. It has also come to my attention that Hammond prosecuted a serial arsonist a few years back who used some pretty unique fire igniters. You wouldn't know anything about how involved he was in the research for that trial, would you?"

I felt all the blood drain from my face. My hands were trembling. I was having a hard time coming to grips with what Morgan was saying to me. And where was Hamm? If I could just talk to him, I was sure all of these awful accusations would be cleared up.

I was trying so hard to focus and remain calm that I didn't notice the golf cart until it came to a stop inches from where we were standing. Sirena stepped out and scanned the scene.

"What's all the excitement? I was heading to my shop when I saw the flames and heard sirens. I came to see what's going on. A girl could start getting paranoid. Is everyone okay?"

She stopped talking and raised her eyebrows in surprise. She looked from June to me, taking in all the details: disheveled torn work uniforms, hair in utter disarray, and of course, the bloody shin, sooty faces and partial mustaches. Considering what we looked like the last time we ran into her, I wondered if she thought our current state was an improvement. To her credit, she didn't mention anything. Instead, she directed her next comments to Detective Morgan.

"What was in that building? I was under the impression it was an empty warehouse. Do you know how the fire started?"

Morgan addressed her questions politely.

"We haven't begun to process the scene, so I don't have anything to report. No one was injured, and I need to clear the area so the firemen and I can get to work here. Could you help me out by giving Francie and June a lift? If it's okay, I'd like for them to wait for me at your shop. I'll be by in a while to tie up some loose ends. These ladies have had enough excitement for one morning."

Sirena smiled at Morgan and agreed. "Anything to help get to the bottom of this. Hop on, girls. I'll take good care of you."

June helped me onto the back seat of Sirena's golf cart where we mutely stared at the receding scene as it disappeared under a soft gray blanket of smoke. Numb with shock, neither of us spoke a word during the short trip to the Jewel of the Bay boutique. My shin was throbbing and my mind was reeling with everything Detective Morgan had told me.

Sirena parked the golf cart on the side drive, walked around to where we still sat motionless on the bench seat, and held out both her hands.

"Come with me, dears. I'll get you settled." Her voice was warm and soothing like whiskey and honey.

She took one of each of our hands and escorted us through the shop door into the cozy sitting area near the back of the store. Two pretty chairs upholstered in watercolor shades were arranged at forty-five degree angles around a coffee table made from local driftwood. As soon as we were seated, Sirena left through a doorway covered by pearlescent curtains I had assumed was a storeroom the first time we visited the boutique. That seemed like years ago. A short while later, she reappeared, carrying a silver tray with warm towels and chilled white wine in laser-etched goblets. She set the tray down on the varnished table top between us and sat in a third chair, this one a straight-back piece painted a rich emerald green and positioned across from us. Sirena looked like she was holding court, posture perfect, hands folded serenely in her lap.

I picked up one of the soft, white towels and dabbed at my shin through the torn fabric of my pant leg. The wound was not as nasty as I had anticipated, and after I wiped away the dried blood and extracted the splinter, it felt much better.

"Ouch!" I gingerly touched my face and winced when I felt the pinch and tug of stage adhesive below my nose. What a sight we must be! Our disguises seemed beyond ridiculous now. How could we explain our get-ups to Sirena without sounding like certifiable idiots? Why did we ever think we could pull off our ludicrous plan?

Rather than cleaning up, June chose the wine. She held the cool goblet to her forehead with both hands after which she lowered it to her lips and tilted her head back. When she set the fancy glass back on the tray, it had a brown swish of a mustache stuck to its rim. We were two ugly ducklings in the royal pond being attended to by the princess swan. Sitting in that beautiful room surrounded by lovely things, we looked at one another and broke out of our state of shocked stupidity. Neither of us was to the point yet of laughing at our foibles, but we were making progress. June turned her gaze to Sirena, who was still sitting peacefully in the chair across from us.

"How can we begin to thank you for everything? You've done so much for us and we hardly know you. I can't imagine what you must be thinking. Let me explain."

"There's no need to explain, June. I've learned since coming here that what goes around comes around. It's important for all of us to keep an eye on one another."

"Well then, let me thank you again. The wine was perfect. Exactly what I needed. In fact, I'd swear it's my favorite Pinot Grigio?Ecco Domani."

Sirena stood up and made a quick trip back to her storeroom. She returned with an open bottle of Ecco Domani.

"Let's toast then." She refilled June's glass, and poured one for herself. We all raised our glasses and said, "Ecco Domani! Here's tomorrow!"

Those two little words would be remembered for a very long time.

I raised my glass and took a sip. The cool wine tickled the back of my throat and snapped me out of the debilitating funk that had me on autopilot since I heard the news about Hamm.

"Sirena, can I bother you for one more thing? May I borrow your cell phone? I lost mine somewhere back in all the confusion. It's probably a pile of ashes by now."

"Of, course, Francie. Anything I can do to help."

She pulled her phone from a deep pocket in her long skirt and handed it to me. I needed to be calm. I needed to talk to Hamm. I needed to find out what was going on.

I pressed the button at the bottom of the phone to activate it and followed the familiar cue, "slide to unlock." I swiped my finger across the screen ready to place my call. When I hit the green phone icon at the bottom of the screen it pulled up the last screen used. It happened to be "Recent Calls," and at the top of the list was a familiar number.

"What the...?" I looked up at Sirena who was standing in the middle of the room. "Sirena, why do you have my husband's personal number in your phone? When and why did you dial this number?"

I didn't want to seem rude after everything she'd done to help us, but I needed to know.

Sirena laughed lightly, and reassured me. "After we all met, I asked Clifton for all your contact numbers. As a businesswoman, this is standard operating procedure. I thought if I got any new merchandise that would help June with her research or got something I thought one of you might like, I could give you or your husband a call. Men are always so clueless when it comes to gift buying. And I understand your husband is not much of a shopper."

When she said this, my brain was flooded once again with all the insinuations flying around about Hammond. How could I help him? I knew in my heart he was innocent, but I had no idea where he was or how to find him. Suddenly, I wasn't feeling all that thankful or trusting toward Sirena or anyone else for that matter. I forced a smile and directed my comment to Sirena.

"Sounds reasonable, I guess. It would be nice if someone gave him a heads up once in a while. Sometimes I get tired of picking out and purchasing my own birthday and anniversary gifts. Thanks for letting me use your phone and for everything else."

I lowered my voice, turned my face away, and dialed my call.

Chapter Twenty-Three

I tried Hamm's cell phone first. It went right to voicemail, and when I tried to leave a message, I was informed by an annoying voice that the mailbox was full.

Next I tried our home phone in case, for some reason, he was there. Maybe he didn't feel well. Maybe, maybe, maybe. This time the voice that answered was my own. I didn't bother to listen to the cheery greeting since I didn't really expect to reach him there. I disconnected call number two.

I saved his office for last. I felt if he were anywhere, this would be the place. His assistant, Liz, answered on the second ring. I wasn't surprised she was in the office, even though it was a holiday weekend; she was young, ambitious, and worked crazy hours because she chose to, not because she was required to.

"I haven't seen him since last Thursday, Francie. He hasn't returned my calls, and he's due in court early tomorrow morning. There's a lot on his agenda right now, and I was hoping to hear from him."

I heard the snap of her gum before she continued. "Quite frankly, I'm getting concerned. This isn't like Mr. Egge. He usually checks in several times a day when he's out of the office."

I knew that. I needed to scream and pound on something, but instead I thanked Liz, disconnected the call, and handed Sirena's phone back to her without a word. I didn't know what to think.

June picked up on the fear and tension in my face. "Sweetie, Hamm's probably running all over town, getting all his work done. You know how he is when he gets focused on something."

Sirena chimed in. "Yes. I bet he's at the courthouse or somewhere preparing for his case. He'll call you back as soon as he can."

What could I do? Absolutely nothing, so I sipped my wine.

Hundreds of unanswered questions and awful, Lifetime TV-inspired scenarios ricocheted inside my skull, adding to the nagging headache I had developed. Something was wrong, but what?

The front door swung open and in strode Detective Jack Morgan. The stern look on his face did not bode well. I wasn't sure how much more of this I could take, but I needed answers. June and I exchanged glances and began firing questions at Morgan.

"Did you find the guy who started the fire?"

"Do you know why he was trying to kill us?"

"Have you found Hamm?"

"Where are Ruby and Roger?"

"Do they know the person who was found in the store?"

"What about the fake merchandise?"

"Did you see my cell phone?"

He never blinked. When we were finished barraging him with questions, he spoke in a measured voice. "Ladies, listen to me. Really listen. What I need from both of you is one thing and one thing only. For me to make any progress on any of this, I need the two of you to get back to Beacon Pointe and stay there. I don't care if you stay at the condo or one of your boats, just stay put. I'll be in touch. Call me if you see or hear from Hammond. Other than that, stay put and let me do my job. I'll come by tomorrow to get complete statements. Until then, don't talk to anyone else, and most importantly, don't go anywhere.

"Sirena, I'd like for you to stick close to home as well. I have a few questions for you too. But first, can you give these two a lift back to Cozy Cove so they can get in their boat and head home? And I do mean straight home."

Sirena's lovely face crinkled into a look I could not decipher, but it vanished as quickly as it had appeared. "Of course I'll take them back, Jack."

"Thank you, Sirena. I appreciate your cooperation and assistance."

"Well then, whenever you're ready, I'll give you girls a lift back in my golf cart."

I was feeling utterly drained and wanted to splash some water on my face. "I'm going to make a quick pit stop before we get on our way."

"Not a problem," Sirena replied. "I'll be right outside. Take your time."

Once inside the powder room meant for clients, I turned on the faucet and cupped my hands under the cool water. When I straightened and reached for the fluffy white towel hanging on a silver ring beside the sink, I was confronted with my reflection in the mirror. It took me by surprise. Staring back at me was the face of my teenage son. Dressed like a grocery delivery man. I made a mental note to advise Ben not to grow a mustache. I finished up, wiped the last of the mustache and adhesive off my face, and hoped I hadn't permanently damaged Sirena's pretty guest towel. Oh, well, right now that was the least of my worries.

Sirena and June were waiting for me outside in her company golf cart. I hopped once again on the rear-facing bench seat next to June, and Sirena put the cart in reverse, turned around in the gravel lot, and headed down the road toward the lake. The ride back to the dock took less than five minutes.

"Here we are," Sirena announced, stopping the vehicle in the small lot of Cozy Cove. June and I hopped off the golf cart and headed toward Lynn's jet boat, which was bobbing at the dock.

"June?" We both turned around. Sirena had followed us down the short dock.

Her arm was outstretched, and in her hand was a small gift bag.

"It's not much," she explained, "but maybe it will help relax you later. It's two samples of my calming lavender-vanilla glycerin soap that I make for special customers. My own secret formula." She smiled sweetly.

June accepted the gift with profuse thanks for all of her kindness. She was about to wrap her arms around Sirena in a no-holds-barred gesture of June-style appreciation, but our new friend took a step back and clasped her hands behind her back.

"Safe journey!" she called brightly to us as we pulled away from the dock.

"She thinks of everything, doesn't she?" June took one of the artfully wrapped bars of soap out of the bag and held it up to my nose so I could keep my hands on the steering wheel.

I inhaled its rich scent and agreed with June's assessment.

"She does indeed. She does indeed."

"I wonder if that list of ingredients you found is stuff she uses to make her soap. I think glycerin was on it, and she said one of the things the soap was made of was glycerin. There weren't that many other things on the list, even though I've never heard of a few of them. If we could figure out the rest of the ingredients, I bet we could make some fantastic-smelling soaps to give out for Christmas gifts. We'll have to ask her about it."

"Mmmmhhh." I was having a hard time envisioning craft time, sitting around the dining room table making fancy soap for Christmas presents when everything around me was in disarray.

I eased out of the slip and set our compass heading in a straight line back to Beacon Pointe. The water was calm and the sun was bright. It could have been a typical summer day, except of course, for our outfits and the fact that someone kept trying to kill us. I looked back to the island, thinking I'd give Sirena a wave and a toot of the boat's horn in a final gesture of thanks.

A soft breeze lifted Sirena's coppery curls off the back of her neck as she drove her golf cart up the gentle incline leading back to her shop. She wouldn't have been able to see us wave, so June and I simply watched her receding figure as it faded out of our view. I recalled thinking she had the ethereal look of a mythical mermaid.

Then the smoke returned. Sirena was being swallowed up by an angry cloud of black smoke. In seconds, she and her vehicle were obliterated from our view. Before either of us had time to speak, our senses were assaulted a second time, but this time it was an ear-splitting explosion. I throttled the jet boat into neutral, then into reverse, in a futile attempt to point my way back to the entrance of the port, but it was no use. By the time I got close enough to re-enter the small port, police and fire rescue vessels were descending on the scene. It's a small island, and news spreads faster than warm butter on a biscuit around here. The only thing left to do was turn back toward our home port. I couldn't imagine what Jack would do if we showed up at the scene of another fire.

June's eyes grew wide. "What's happening? More smoke and fire. It seems like it's following us, trying to choke or swallow us everywhere we go."

"I don't know. I feel like I'm stuck in a bad script and all the writers are on strike. No one is safe from this mysterious miscreant. What if Sirena's hurt? I would never be able to live with the guilt, wondering if we were the actual targets all along."

"I hate to admit it, Francie, but we kind of suck at this whole investigating thing. Maybe Morgan was right. Maybe we should lock ourselves behind closed doors until this is all over."

"But we can't sit back and let this maniac carry on. We don't know why he wants us dead. He must have seen you the day after the fire at Ruby's when he was talking to Roger. I guess you were right to be suspicious. All we can do now is keep trying to prove this man is setting fire to everything in his path in order to cover his knock-off selling ass. We can't let him hurt anyone else close to us."

"I'm going to try calling Sirena. I need to make sure she's alright. I don't want to hear about it on the six o'clock news."

June retrieved her cell phone which had miraculously survived. Unfortunately, her expensive camera containing all the pictures she took of the evidence to support our theories had been destroyed. We were back to square one.

Chapter Twenty-Four

I watched as June tried repeatedly to get a connection through to Sirena. Everything was surreal. It was the kind of day you dreamed about all winter long during Ohio's endless weeks of frigid temperatures and drifting snow. The early-summer sun warmed our faces and shoulders and made the calm waters of Lake Erie sparkle. For a moment, it was possible to forget the sight of that black cloud lingering along a section of the shoreline. The casual observer wouldn't think twice about it. It could have been someone's first attempt at a summer barbecue. We knew however that it represented an attempt of a very different kind.

I continued steering the boat toward our home port as June disconnected the failed call one last time and tossed her phone on the floor of the boat in frustration.

"It went straight to voicemail."

"I'm sure she's okay. We'll hear from her soon."

"I hope you're right. I have so many questions and no answers. Do you think the golf cart explosion was aimed at us? I mean, we were riding on it minutes before Sirena took off."

"I don't know. This cloak-and-dagger stuff isn't at all fun in real life. I'm just glad we are off the island and almost back to the marina."

Weekend boaters were all around us. June looked at the happy people on the water taking advantage of the long Memorial Day holiday. There would be plenty of sunburned shoulders and noses tonight, but chances are, not too many people would be complaining.

"I bet we're going to be the only ones around here tonight sifting through clues, trying to figure out the who and why of all these attempts at burning us down, blowing us up, or drowning us."

I had to agree. "The only thing we have to be thankful for is that the person responsible for our trouble seems to be even more inept than us at carrying out his plans."

For a while things got quiet. Not feeling the need for any more excitement, I kept my speed to a minimum, deep in thought, replaying all the disconnected events from the past twenty-four hours and trying to fit together some of the puzzle pieces that must interlock to explain the big picture: the tragic fire at Ruby's, the horrific discovery of the unknown homicide victim in the attic, the stranger, and the second fire at the warehouse. Then there was the fact both June and Michael had turned up unconscious on the beach and not least of all, Hamm's inexplicable absence. Something sinister was going on, but what? And how did we all fit into the mix? Were we just unwilling participants in a heinous scheme or was there something more personal going on here?

June snapped me out of my reverie with a warning. "Look out, Francie. Turn!"

Cranking the steering wheel to the right, I narrowly missed being rammed on the port side by a rider on a shiny, black Jet Ski. This guy, dressed in a black, full-body, neoprene wetsuit complete with skull-hugging hood, was not jumping wakes for some afternoon jollies.

I straightened the boat and was beginning to readjust my heading when June's blood curdling scream knifed through my brain and sent me into survival mode.

"He's got a gun!"

I turned my head in time to see the ghastly rider gripping the controls of his watercraft with one hand, and with his other arm outstretched, pointing a gun directly at us.

I jammed the throttle forward with everything I had.

"Hang on, June!"

Grabbing the side of the boat, June flattened herself and hung on for dear life. This could not be happening again!

A bullet whizzed by, missing me by inches. I could actually hear it. I wanted to crumple into a pile of whimpering, gasping terror. I needed someone to take care of me, to fix this. But there was no one; there was only me. So I did the only thing I could think of. I screamed. And screamed. And screamed.

Over the sound of my own wailing, I realized June was also screaming. Our screams turned into a fractured, squealing language that only the very best of friends could understand. Two things became certain: we were both terrified, and neither of us had anything even closely resembling a plan. The best I could do was continue full speed ahead, weaving back and forth through the water and other vessels so our pursuer could not get a straight shot at us, at the same time hoping someone would recognize what was happening and call 911.

Another bullet barely missed us, smashing into a nearby metal buoy with a metallic clang. I ventured a swift glance behind me and saw June still braced on the floor of the boat with her head practically inside my purse. She was silent. I did a double take, checking to make sure all of her body parts were attached and intact, which I was happy to see they were.

"June, please, you've got to think of something before we are both killed!"

June lifted her face from the floor revealing a calm, determined expression; her fists were clenched around several mysterious objects. "Slow down and let Mr. Psycho catch up to us."

"What? No way! You must have hit your head and forgotten what's happening here. We're trying to get away from this nut, not invite him aboard for snacks."

"Just do it. I have a plan."

With great trepidation, I eased up on the throttle. "This better be good, June, because otherwise, if we don't die, I might have to kill you."

"Trust me. I've got this."

I shrugged. "Well, that's more than I can say for myself. I've got nothing."

What she had in her hands turned out to be a smoke bomb left over from last Fourth of July, a book of matches from the Island House, and the tube of mustache adhesive we had used this morning when we still thought we were clever.

Maintaining a moderate speed, I scanned the area, keeping the Jet Ski in my sight. It was getting closer. I was getting nervous.

"Whatever magic you have up your sleeve, you better do it now before it's too late."

After coating the smoke bomb in a thick layer of mustache adhesive, June struck a match and lit the wick.

Our persistent pursuer was now on our starboard side, perfectly matching our pace and heading. His right hand was raised. While maneuvering with his left, he pointed the gun ready to deliver his fatal shot. I figured my fate was sealed, but all I could do was grip the throttle. June stood up, leaned slightly back for balance, wound up and let it rip.

"Banzai!" She screamed like a woman possessed.

Her creation landed spot on between the goon's handlebars thanks to ten years of pitching on the freelance journalists' co-ed softball team. A curtain of smoke shrouded our attacker and his ride within seconds, and as we pulled away from the spot of impact, we looked back to see the Jet Ski lazily bobbing in the water minus one crazy rider. This time smoke had been on our side.

"Home run!"

"That was epic! I love you!"

We high-fived each other in delirious relief. We screamed again, but this time we were whooping in triumph. I smashed the throttle forward, and our wake was a glorious sight as we bee-lined back to the safety of Beacon Pointe, the marina, and my cozy condo.

The entire nightmare ride had taken only fifteen minutes. We reached the marina, and I docked the jet boat safely back in Lynn's slip. June gathered up our gear and scooped up the contents of my purse, returning things to a semblance of normalcy. In less than the time it would take to watch an episode of Everybody Loves Raymond, we had nearly died for the second time in as many days. When my feet hit the solid dock, I had to force myself not to bend down and kiss the ground. This latest adventure may have only lasted a few minutes, but I think it scared ten years off of my life.

"Don't you think now is a good time to call in reinforcements? Let's let the police take over this mess. Having so recently cheated the grim reaper out of his daily quota, it seemed like the proper thing to do.

Chapter Twenty-Five

When I opened the kitchen door to the condo, I expected to be run over by a dog with only one thing on his mind. We had been gone much longer than expected, and I had no idea what Gunner's potty schedule was. I hoped we weren't too late. The only thing that greeted us, however, was silence. I called out Gunner's name, but no furry, tail-wagging dog appeared. He was gone. I was about to tell June when I saw she was slipping her cell phone back into her pocket and had a confused look on her face.

"What is it, June? Was that the police? Are they going to help us now?"

"He's gone. Michael is gone. I called to check on him, and the receptionist said he disappeared without being discharged. At least we know he's awake."

"What? And I'm sure you noticed Gunner is gone too. Michael must have been here and found him. He was here Saturday night when we brought you back from the beach, and I get the feeling he wouldn't have much trouble getting inside again, even without a key. I hope at least they are together."

"Francie, maybe we should hold off calling the cops until we find out what happened to Michael and Gunner. I have a feeling all this is connected."

And so we got back to the business of pretending all was well. By the time June and I were showered, dried and fluffed, it was late afternoon. We hadn't eaten anything since our grilled cheese sandwiches at the Cozy Cove. That seemed so long ago now, and I realized I was hungry.

"I can't think about cooking right now, and I'm not in the mood for another pizza. Let's grab a bite at the Tiki Table. Chicken and cheese quesadillas sound pretty good, and they make a marvelous margarita."

"I could use a margarita. I think I'm dehydrated." June sucked in her cheeks, puckered her lips, then made a loud smacking sound. "Let's take the car. I'm running out of energy."

I was glad to hear June's suggestion. I wasn't planning to admit my calves were burning, my shin was tender and sore, my right elbow was bruised and throbbing, and the kink in my neck was preventing me from turning my head to the left.

We made the five-minute trip across the resort property from the condo to the beach where the Tiki Table was located. The private, casual, outdoor-dining restaurant facing the lake was meant to provide the perfect spot for Beacon Pointe members to relax and wind down after a long day in the sun.

We reached the eatery just as the sun was making its way toward the horizon beyond the sandy beach. Diehard sunbathers, not wanting to miss out on the final rays, begrudgingly packed their beach bags.

June and I lucked out and scored a great table on the patio overlooking the breathtaking scenery.

"I could sit here forever and never get tired of this view." I sighed contentedly as I stretched my tired legs out in front of me and kneaded the tight muscles in my shoulders with my fingertips.

"After the day we had, they might have to toss us a pillow before they lock up for the night. Unfortunately, my editor is expecting me to email him an update on the progress of my article. I don't know where to begin with that. Luckily, I uploaded the pictures I took at Ruby's before the fire to my tablet and cell phone, and the ones from Jewel of the Bay as well. The basic article won't take long to put together. The ones I needed most though are gone. We could have probably gotten to the bottom of this with the pictures I took at the warehouse."

"Wow. That's a tough one. It was supposed to be a lighthearted summer piece, but now you can't ignore the fire and the attempted murders and the body in the attic. Do you think your editor will want to print that story?"

"It doesn't fit with the personality of this particular magazine, but he has other publications that would want it. How can I write something like that though? We're still in the middle of this mess. Who knows how it's all going to end?"

"Well, I think we're in over our heads. I was right before. We need to let the professionals handle the crime-solving from here on."

June nodded in agreement, lifted her weary hand, and wiggled her graceful fingers in the direction of a waitress who scurried by, balancing a tray of drinks at shoulder level while avoiding collisions with co-workers, patrons, and children running back and forth between the beach, their parents, and French fries.

When the sure-footed young woman made it back to our table, she offered us menus and asked for our drink orders.

"I think I'll pass on margaritas for now. What do you think, June? Do you want to split a bottle of wine instead?"

"That sounds good to me."

"I'll be right back with your drinks, ladies."

While we waited for our wine to arrive, I checked out the menu, and June scrolled through the photos on her phone.

"Hmm, this is interesting. Look, Francie." She pinched her fingers on the center of a picture then spread them outward to enlarge the image. "What does this look like to you?"

"It looks like the inside of Ruby's store. What am I supposed to be seeing?"

"Look closer. There. The window. What is that outside the back window?"

I took June's phone and held it up to my face, focusing on the window. "It's a boat trailer. So what? There's nothing unusual about that."

"Except it's not a boat. It's a Jet Ski. A black Jet Ski."

"Yes, I see it, but that doesn't prove anything. We are on an island, and every third person owns a Jet Ski or a speed boat."

"I'm just saying. That's all. Oh screw it. Let's share the 'Mamma Mia's Dish of Love.'"

How could I refuse?

The wine arrived, accompanied by two stemless wine glasses etched with the restaurant logo. June placed our food order for us, and after the waitress walked off, she raised her glass and offered a toast.

"Well, here's to surviving the day," she said with the smallest hint of sarcasm in her voice. We clinked glasses and sipped.

We were on our second glass when the overflowing platter of cheeses, fruits, Italian bread and olives was placed on the center of the table, taking up almost all of the available space. I reached for a Kalamata olive and a strawberry; June chose a healthy hunk of bread, smeared it with butter, and added a slab of cheese for good measure.

"Oh what the heck. Pass the bread please."

After enjoying the comfort food for a while, it was time to bring up the topic both of us were avoiding.

"Okay, June, now we can talk. I still haven't heard from Hamm, and frankly, I don't know how much longer I can pretend that everything is fine. Even though my phone is probably a pile of "i-Ashes" by now, he still knows how to get a hold of me. I mean, he could call the marina office, leave a message on the condo machine, or he could break down and call your cell phone for goodness sake. I know something's wrong."

"I agree. This is highly unusual behavior for the Egg. You have to admit, though, we haven't exactly been checking in ourselves or checking messages lately for that matter. Seriously, what could be wrong? I mean, it's not like some evil mastermind has abducted him and is holding him captive in his island lair. It's bad timing, sweetie. You two will connect soon, and you'll realize that you've just been reading way too many bad mystery scripts this year. But beyond that, what do you think happened to Sirena and her golf cart? Was it a backfiring muffler, or was it an attempt to get rid of her? Or us for that matter. That was a loud boom and a lot of smoke for a golf cart malfunction."

"I know, I know. Too much doesn't feel right about this to me. How did our annual Memorial Day fun, sun, and shopping weekend turn into such a mess?"

June shook her head and replied, "I don't know, but even though we can't seem to avoid daily attempts on our lives, there is one thing we do exceptionally well, and that is coming up with plans. We need a good one this time for figuring out who this bad guy is. Let's get to the bottom of this mystery, so we can lie back in our beach chairs and get to the bottom of a margarita instead."

"Now that sounds like a happy ending! Let me find my notebook and a pen so we can get organized."

So much for leaving the investigation to the professionals. I hauled my tote bag onto my lap and dug around, producing a hot pink pad of rule-lined paper and a nice variety of colored gel pens.

"Okay, I'm ready. Let's start from the beginning. What do we know? We have to get the who, what, when, where, why and how."

"Oh boy, now you sound like my journalism instructor. I always forget you were an English teacher before you became fun. I'll bite though. I think the *who* is knock-off guy, maybe even a partner, or the mob. The *what* seems to be some sort of cover-up. The *when*, well, that's pretty much anytime we turn around, and that's also the where—anywhere we happen to be. The *why* is the big one. I guess he could be covering up a 'knock-off scheme' like we first thought. Or maybe he has been supplying the island with fake designer items for years making a fortune on phony merchandise, and maybe someone, probably Ruby and Roger, figured out what he was up to. He panicked and destroyed their store and all of their merchandise so they would have no proof of his crimes. What do you think?"

"I don't know. And what about that poor victim they found burnt in the attic? Does anyone know who that might be? I still can't get my mind around a diabolical scheme centering around our favorite vacation spot and our good friends."

I had a vision of evil fiends skulking around in the dark with engraved lighters waiting for their chance to carry out an evil plot. Shaking my head and twisting my hair into a messy knot gave me time to rid myself of negative thoughts and consider the possibilities.

"Do you think Ruby and Roger could be in some kind of financial trouble?" I conjectured. "Maybe they had no choice but to buy the knock-offs and try to charge full price for them."

"It's hard to say what people, even good ones, will do in a financial crisis. I guess it could happen. So, what do you think we should do, Francie? Do you have a magic wand or a crystal ball in that bag of yours? We need something to point us in the right direction. How are we going to find out who this guy is?"

"I say we lay a trap for him. We know he's been following us. Let's stick around here until he comes back. Then we can ambush him. I have some pepper spray somewhere in my purse, and I know you've been training with that good-looking instructor at the Tae Kwon Do studio, if you could call that training... I'm sure between the two of us and our super skills, we could hold that poorly dressed, ponytailed greaser down until we can call your Detective Morgan for backup."

"He's not mine yet, but here's to hoping. From what I gather, he is unattached and available, and he is definitely too dreamy to be hiding away on the island all alone."

"All right, Aphrodite, cool your toga! Do you think it's doable? Can we actually pull this one off? Up until now, our track record hasn't been all that great."

"Well, we have to try to do something to end this nightmare. I can't take one more day of this craziness, and I'm ready to give this everything I've got."

"Me too. I can't stand not knowing where Hamm is, and the fires and explosions are starting to get old."

Chapter Twenty-Six

We spent the rest of our time sipping our wine and savoring the last of our meal. Occasionally, one of us would suggest a strategy detail or a slight addition to the basic plan, but we couldn't come up with any better alternative, so we decided to go with it, determined to make it happen.

June and I left the patio and headed toward the marina and June's houseboat. There was no turning back now. Mission Find the Bad Guy was under way. Once we got aboard Anchor Management, we set about making as much noise as we could, dropping cups and dishes into the sink, flinging notebooks, talking loudly and laughing as if we were having a grand old time. June strode fore to aft turning on all of the lights in the cabin. This was to make our whereabouts obvious to anyone who happened to be watching us.

"So now what?" she asked, kicking aside a pile of magazines and a small recorder that had landed in front of the sink where she now stood with her arms crossed in front of her.

"I say we pop in a DVD, microwave some popcorn, and wait."

"That's the hardest part, just sitting around. What if no one shows up?" Inactivity had never been June's strong suit.

Soon, we were caught up in our favorite movie, Thelma and Louise. For the next half hour, we shared popcorn and got inspired by Susan Sarandon and Geena Davis making tracks in their '66 Thunderbird. But before Brad Pitt made his getaway with all the money, it was time to make our move. The night had turned inky dark. The kind that only occurs far away from streetlights and convenience store neon signs. We changed into solid black shirts and pants. Knowing how I always get chilly in the night air, I also borrowed a black, hooded sweatshirt with the yacht club insignia embroidered tastefully on the front pocket. Lucky for me, June had stretchy black leggings in addition to her size-two jeans. We both wear size-eight shoes, and being the fashionista she is, June had tall black boots as well as ankle booties in her closet. I pulled the knee-high boots over the leggings and admired my new look in the full-length mirror attached to the back of the door to the forward berth. I don't mind saying that I looked pretty cool and mysterious. I conveniently had a tin of black shoe polish stashed in my bag. Sometimes, I had to give Hamm's dress shoes a quick shine before an important engagement. After all these years, he was still fussy about the condition of his shoes. We dipped our fingers into the greasy stuff and smudged a bit under each eye. We pulled black ball caps over our hair and our ensembles were complete.

"Stay low," June whispered as we exited the boat and crept stealthily down the length of the dock, making our way to the little patch of trees and tall ornamental grass at the end. When we got to our hiding spot, we crouched down and held our breath for what seemed like hours. I took a quick peek at my watch and discovered only fifteen minutes had passed. In that time, we had seen only two cars and not one single person on foot.

"This is lame. Let's give it up. Once again, what were we thinking?"

June shushed me for the second time in less than one hour. "Listen. I think I hear someone coming."

That someone was tall and dressed very much like the two of us, right down to the black ball cap. "I think it's him, and he has something in his hand, a flashlight, I think."

I was certain it was the knock-off guy. We waited impatiently until the stranger had made it past our hiding place and halfway down the dock before untangling ourselves from the foliage, ready to follow. Before we got to our feet, the perfectly groomed Clifton Sterling appeared, seemingly out of nowhere, and he was walking very purposefully straight toward us.

"What is he doing here?" June squeaked.

It was my turn to shush her. He passed right by us without even a cursory glance and turned onto the dock.

"I think he's going to your boat. Maybe he left something aboard."

"There's nothing of his left there. No. Something's wrong. I can feel it."

Before June could call out a warning to her ex-husband, he had caught up to the mystery person. They stopped right in front of June's boat, and when the stranger in black turned toward Clifton, his eyes widened in recognition. I couldn't hear what he was saying, but his body language told me he was agitated, perhaps even angry. Clifton took a solid hold on the person's left arm. There was a brief struggle. The stranger swung around and smashed the flashlight across the back of Clifton's head. He crumpled to the dock like a marionette whose strings had been cut, and the next sound we heard was the splash of his body as he was nudged by a black steel-tipped boot over the edge of the dock into the water.

I grabbed June's shoulder. She was frozen to her spot, staring wide-eyed at the unfolding scene. "Snap out of it!" I hissed into her ear.

We sprinted toward the spot that Clifton had recently occupied. My raised hand was clutching a can of pepper spray, and June's fists of fury were clenched in front of her, ready to pounce.

The dark figure in front of the houseboat turned resolutely toward us. A feeble moonbeam illuminated the face of Sirena Divine.

"Well, hello, ladies. I must admit I'm surprised. I thought you two were inside having a movie night. Instead, I see you were out playing super spy again. No matter, as long as we're all together now."

"What's going on, Sirena?" I shrieked. "We need to get Clifton out of the water! He's going to drown."

"That's the point, darling. Why don't we all go aboard and have a chat. I can see you haven't put all the pieces together yet." She bent down and called out in an unholy voice that sent a shiver down my spine, "Hey, Cliff, say hello to Hammond when you get to the other side!"

The blood in my veins turned to frozen sludge. Please don't let this be happening!

Sirena straightened up and raised her right hand toward us. What I had thought was a flashlight turned out to be a small black gun with a silver handle. She pointed it at us, and in a sickeningly sweet voice, invited us to join her on June's boat. What choice did we have?

When we got inside, Sirena kept the gun pointed squarely at us and hissed, "Sit down and don't say a single word. Now!"

We slumped on the couch, terrified at the transformation that had turned our gracious new friend into this cold, steely-eyed stranger who was now maniacally rifling through the fridge and cupboards, flinging everything we hadn't thrown earlier across the room.

"Well come on, ladies. Aren't you going to at least offer me a glass of wine so we can chat civilly before I have to kill you? Oh wait, I almost forgot, we drank your bottle of Pinot Grigio at the shop earlier today. Thanks for that by the way. I grabbed it as an afterthought on my way out of here the other night. It turned out to be a pretty good wine. And what was the translation of its name again? Oh, I remember, 'Here's Tomorrow.' Well you won't have to worry about that now."

This time, neither of us became mute with terror. Adrenaline and the instinct to survive set us both into action. June and I started shooting questions at our captor. "What is going on, Sirena? Have you gone crazy?"

"We need to help Clifton and find the knock-off guy!"

"We have to clear Hamm's name and solve the mystery of the fire at Ruby's. Why are you here?"

"And what's with the gun and the threats? We didn't do anything! The real criminal is still out there somewhere."

"Oh, where to start with the questions?" Sirena's calmness now was the exact opposite of her agitated state moments earlier. "You ladies have it all wrong. Some detectives you turned out to be. If I had realized you were so naive and stupid, it might not have been necessary to get rid of you."

She bent down and opened the cupboard under the sink. Never moving her gun away from its targets, she retrieved a bottle of red wine June had stashed there for emergencies. She unscrewed the cap and poured out three servings into red solo cups that she found in the same cupboard, intended for the same purpose.

"Here, have a drink with me while I explain. Then, unfortunately for you, we have to get back to the business of getting you both out of the picture. It's too bad. You seem like you might have been kind of fun."

I held out my shaking hand to take the drink being offered and June did the same. Neither of us could stop staring wide-eyed at Sirena as she paced feverishly back and forth in the tight cabin quarters. She had a disconnected look as she stepped over, around, and on all of the debris cluttering the small space.

"Listen, Sirena, we have got to get out of here. You don't understand..."

She cut me off mid-sentence. "My name is not Sirena! God, how I hate that name. And it is not me who doesn't understand, it is you two bumbling morons!"

She stopped abruptly, set her drink on the counter, and put her hands on her hips. She spoke now through clenched teeth, enunciating every word. "My name is Senora. Sirena is dead. Could you not tell the difference? Sirena was my twin, and I took care of her just like I'm about to take care of you. She was a do-gooder, always interfering in other people's business, just like you. It's no surprise you all hit it off."

"Whaaaat?" I shot to the edge of my seat while June sank farther back into the cushions.

"I don't know what you've been smoking, Sirena, but knock it off. We're fishing Clifton's waterlogged Armani ass out of that water and calling Detective Morgan right now!"

The last thing I saw before being sucked into total oblivion was the lovely Sirena Divine whirling toward me with the half-empty wine bottle.

Chapter Twenty-Seven

I didn't know if I was out for ten minutes or ten hours, but when I tried to open my eyes, they felt as if burning needles were piercing my retinas. My ribs were sore and my head was throbbing. Something warm and sticky was congealing in my hair above my left ear. I was lying on a hard surface and a chilly breeze was sliding over my sore cheeks.

Very slowly, the blurred images around me began to take shape. June was at the helm of her houseboat, standing very stiff and looking very nervous. The hatch above the galley table was open, and the breeze I felt on my face was increasing in intensity. Wait. The boat was moving! But that was impossible. Although it was seaworthy, June's houseboat had never left the dock, at least not under her power. She used the boat strictly as a summertime getaway, a place to kick back, relax, and enjoy leisure times at the dock with her friends. She couldn't actually drive the thing to save her life. I must still be dreaming.

The gun in Sirena's hand, though, was very, very, real. Wait. What had she told us? That wasn't Sirena. What did she say her name was? I was confused, but regardless of the madwoman's name, her gun was pressing into June's side, which explained why she looked so uncomfortable. I was trying not to move or make any noise so I could clear my head and take stock of the situation, but after a few minutes of conscious effort, I could no longer tolerate keeping still on the cold, galley floor. I raised my hand, feeling for broken ribs, then gingerly touched the egg-sized lump on my head. Tears threatened to spill out of my eyes, my mouth was as dry as the sand on the beach, and my nose itched. Concentrating, I stretched my legs out slowly in front of me, trying not to attract attention, but needing to get the blood flowing again. Cautiously, I flexed my ankles and pointed my toes.

Sirena's unnaturally low monotone voice halted my progress.

"I see you've woken up from your siesta, Francesca. Stand up. Now."

The gun, which was now pointed dead center at my belly, got my immediate attention. I swallowed fiercely, trying to keep the stinging bile from making its way up my esophagus, and put all my remaining energy into rearranging my posture into an upright position. My immediate surroundings swirled around me like a 70's psychedelic funhouse; voices were assaulting my ears, bouncing off the walls of some invisible tunnel; and when I tried to speak, all I could manage was a pathetic scratchy, squeak which sounded more like an abandoned kitten than a woman in charge of her own destiny. I managed to pull myself up to a sitting position, clinging to the edge of the galley bench seat for support. It took every ounce of concentration to hold my bobble-head still and focus my eyes on my best friend, trying to eliminate the crazy lady from my line of sight.

June caught my gaze as I painfully whispered, "June, what in God's name is happening here?"

Her ghost-white face was streaked with tears, mascara, and shoe polish. "I think this might be the final act, Francie. This is not Sirena, and there is no hero waiting in the wings. Just do what she says, and maybe we will have a chance to get out of this alive."

"Shut up! Just shut up, you two drama queens!" Sirena's evil incarnation whirled around and stalked out of the cabin. Through the open sliding glass door, I saw her holding on to the rail and looking up into the dark starless night.

Directing her voice back toward us in the cabin, she commanded, "Stop here, June." Senora's order left no room for discussion or compromise. June pulled back on the throttle and gave me a fearful glance. Senora ducked her head back inside for a second, then instructed in a voice as cold as ice, "All right, all hands on deck, girls. And I mean now!"

June slouched out of the captain's chair, terror emanating from her every pore, stepped over to where I stood on shaking legs, and slid her arm protectively around me to help me get my balance. I offered up a silent prayer in thanksgiving for the friend I knew would die trying to save me. The boat bobbed gently from side to side in the dark water, which wasn't helping the fact I was still wobbly and disoriented. After helping me straighten up, we clung to one another, and together we walked the short distance out onto the deck where our captor was waiting. I mustered my courage.

"What have you done to Sirena, you witch?"

"She's dead. I told you. She couldn't keep her interfering nose out of my affairs, so I did what had to be done. I made sure she was in Ruby's shop when it burnt." There was not the slightest hint of remorse in her voice.

I grabbed June's hand. We stood in shocked silence for a second then, in unison, let out a sigh of disbelief, "Noooo!"

Anger boosted my courage to confront her. "How could you? She was your sister. Why would you do these horrible things?"

"Why? For what was coming to me. For what I deserved. For the money that should have been mine. Sirena always had it so easy. She was the golden child, loved by everyone, and everything she touched turned into a success. I had to scratch and claw for every scrap, and no one ever appreciated me, not even my geriatric husband. I had to tolerate that idiot until he died of natural causes, so I could finally enjoy the fortune I had earned. Even after he was dead and buried, I had to fight and scrape to get any of Jerry's estate. It all should have been mine. I'm the one who smiled at his side, kept track of all his pills, cleaned the drool off his chin, and worst of all, put up with his ridiculous friends.

"But no. It was unbelievable. He cut me out of his will in the end and left everything: his money, his house, his four cars, and all of his assets to his buddies who shared his bizarre fascination. Come on! The Naked Jugglers' Foundation? I wasted ten years of my life only to have it all yanked away by those morons. But I discovered one important oversight on the part of his legal counsel. My dear hubby's treasured coin collection didn't get itemized or catalogued with his other assets. It would have ended up being auctioned off by those flipping fools anyway."

We needed to keep her talking until we could come up with something resembling a counter attack. June asked, "What about the guy in black who keeps trying to kill us? And didn't he try to blow you up as well? Obviously he wasn't successful, but he can't be your loyal partner."

"Oh, you've met my friend, Kenneth. He doesn't look like a brain trust, but he does have a few redeeming qualities. He agreed to help me steal Jerry's coin stash before the error could be discovered, and it wound up for sale, or worse yet, donated to the juggling jerk-offs. Overmayer has some pretty solid connections out East. He knows some professionals who could help us liquidate the coins into lovely, spendable cash, and the rest, as they say, is history. With the backing of my new friends, I invested in a booming business moving very authentic-looking designer merchandise all over the Midwest."

June and I were incredulous. She was first to ask the question that was foremost on my mind. "You were the one selling all those knock-offs? But how?"

I was slowly regaining my focus. My adrenaline had caught up with my fear and anger, and the creative juices were starting to flow again. I had spotted my purse wedged between a chair and a table leg just inside the cabin door. It must have landed there while I was being knocked out and kicked around. I angled my body so I was partially behind June, and while she kept the crazy lady engaged in conversation, I carefully stretched my right leg through the open cabin door. I wedged the toe of my shoe under the shoulder strap and painstakingly nudged the bag, willing it to move closer to the door.

"So, you were willing to kill not only your husband, but also your own twin sister, just to get rich? Was it worth it, Senora?"

"Oh, it was worth it. Profits were just starting to roll in on a regular basis. I was already pushing my wares in tourist towns up and down Lake Michigan. I was working from my home base in Chicago. Once I had that market under control, it was time to expand into Lake Erie. I could kill two birds with one stone, so to speak. Little Miss Perfect had unknowingly laid the groundwork for me with her new island boutique. And for once, I was glad we were identical in appearance. I was delighted when I saw her beautiful tattoo. How convenient for me. It's an exact mirror image of my own."

Senora lifted her black tee shirt to reveal rock-hard abs, a sexy black bra, and an intricate, richly colored scorpion winding its way across her chest.

An image of our evening at the Island House flashed through my mind. I remembered having a fleeting sense that night that something was off. Now, it was crystal clear. The tattoo, the martini, the change in attitude. It was her all along. But I couldn't figure out how Senora had taken her sister's place at the Island House. All I could picture in my mind was that strange look on Sirena's face as she checked her phone on her way inside the building. It was a combination of fear and excitement, but it didn't matter now. No one might ever discover the truth, at least no one who would live to tell the story.

Senora smoothed her shirt back over her toned body and continued her story in a trance-like monologue. For the time being, she seemed to forget that we were there.

"Once I got Sirena out of my way, which by the way, was entirely too easy, I had the perfect opportunity to start slipping my counterfeit designer goods in with real deliveries all over Kelleys Island. There were lots of products too, not just fashion accessories. I had a nice business going on with the pharmacies as well. Make-up, hair care products, heck, I even had counterfeit prescription drugs. There's a pretty big market for cheap Viagra around here. It probably doesn't work, but that's not my concern."

I remembered one of the red-circled newspaper articles in Michael's backpack. It was about an FBI sting uncovering a network of underworld counterfeiters operating out of Chicago and New York. This was starting to make some sense now.

The crazy lady continued her story. "I had a nice little export business going using Overmayer as my front man, but now that Sirena was gone, I could begin to openly do business myself and get things done much more quickly and efficiently. I had already made contacts at Put-In-Bay and some of the mainland retail and drug establishments and everything was lined up. My dreams were about to come true."

She stopped talking then. The moment had passed. Senora was back in the present, and she stared at us with menacing eyes.

"It was perfect. Things were progressing exactly as I had planned until you two Nancy Drews started to interfere."

June threw out one last-ditch attempt to keep her distracted while I tried to get at my handbag, with the faint hope I could manage to come up with something that might buy us some time.

"How did you do it, Senora? I mean, how did you trade places with your sister, right under our noses? You must be a real pro at this criminal stuff. It took a lot of nerve trying something like that right in front of a real detective!"

June must have struck a chord, appealing to Senora's twisted vanity because she jumped at the chance to extol her evil skills.

"Oh, that law man has nothing on me. You all made it way too easy. I sent my clueless sister a text message instructing her to meet me in front of Inscription Rock. It was an emergency, and she should come right away. No time for good-byes. We hadn't spoken in eight years, and that brainless fool actually thought I wanted to see her and have a little family reunion. What I wanted, though, was to give her a permanent going away party."

"But if it was you who joined us after dinner, how did you know what to wear? You were dressed exactly like Sirena."

"I am a very patient and methodical person. I have been working my plan in the shadows for a very long time now. It amazes me how oblivious everyone is around here. No one locks their doors. People trust their neighbors. I walked in and out of Sirena's house so many times while she was at work, and no one ever questioned me. Instead, they waved to me! It was easy to sneak into her room and inventory her closet and drawers. I even copied her shampoo, soap, make-up, and perfume in case I needed to cozy up to her new boyfriend. After old decrepit Jerry, Mr. Sterling might have been a nice change of pace. I never did get the chance to find out.

"It was lucky for me Sirena was so gung-ho on supporting the local economy. Nearly everything she owned came from local vendors or else she made it herself. I'll miss her hand-made soaps and lotions. They were actually very good. And the chocolate. Oh the chocolate! I thought it was very generous of me to share some of her last products with you, don't you agree? Sorry about the little mix-up at the vendor display. No harm no fowl, right?"

Understanding oozed into my consciousness. June was not the intended target of whatever was infused into the special box of chocolates. She was just collateral damage. I had a memory flash of a crumpled wrapper in the backpack of the person looking into nefarious transactions and mob connections.

"For the rest of her belongings, I simply made sure to purchase my duplicate items on different shifts than the ones she shopped. And then I watched. You two aren't the only ones who can master a passable disguise."

"Can't you please let us go? We won't tell anyone about this, and you can just disappear. No one else has to be hurt." June's last-ditch effort seemed to have run its course. It looked like the conversation was about to end for good.

"It's too late for that now. Sirena is dead. Clueless Clifton will soon be making his way to Davy Jones' Locker. If he hasn't drowned by now, it won't take long for him to die of hypothermia, and Francie, your darling Hammond's body should be discovered in the old fish gutting shanty near the docks on the island's north end one of these days. Once the two of you disappear, good old Detective Morgan might have his suspicions, but he'll never be able to put all of the pieces together or prove I was connected to any of it, and I will be in the clear forever.

"Then, I'll just need to tie up the final loose end. I'll schedule an intimate cocktail party with Kenneth to celebrate our success. He'll be so flattered. He's been salivating after me like a dog in heat since we first met back in Chicago. One quick drink laced with a bit of one of my secret recipes, and I'll have no one left to connect me with anything. I'll have to tweak my recipe a bit, since both my trial runs were just short of success. I still can't believe that idiot thought he could blow me up on my own golf cart and get away with the money. He could never outsmart me. As soon as I smelled the telltale sweet odor of my fire accelerant, I knew what he was up to and jumped off the moving cart before it caught fire and blew up.

"Anyway, enough of all that. None of it will matter soon. I think it's time for you to take your final curtain call. Get over to the edge of the boat, ladies."

This was my last chance. I was probably going to die, but I wasn't going down without a fight.

I pretended to trip and stumble over the deck chair, falling purposely into the doorway to the cabin. The trip was staged, but the shooting pain in my hip was very real when I made contact with the deck boards. I only had a few seconds to reach into my handbag and grab the first things I felt. I couldn't see what I had clutched in my hand, and even if I could, I didn't have time to be picky. It felt like a paperback novel and possibly a set of keys. I shoved the items into the front pocket of my borrowed sweatshirt, and scooted out of the doorway, reluctantly joining June, who was stepping out onto the narrow swim platform on the back of the boat.

"Okay, ladies, it has been great catching up and all, but I still have so much to do tonight. It's time for you to go for your final swim."

"Please, Senora! We'll drown out here in the middle of the lake. Or die of hypothermia. What about my children? They're going to be orphans if the horrible things you said about Hamm are true." I wasn't acting now; I was begging. My voice was getting weak, and I was trembling.

"Oh, the possibilities! Sadly, I'll be gone before I can find out the final cause of your 'accidental' deaths. And about your kids—don't worry. They will find a way to survive. It's ironic, don't you think, they being twins and all. I wonder which one will end up with all the power."

"They're not like you!" I screamed right in her face. "They are nothing like you. They are kind and good. They love each other and take care of each other."

"Well, there you go, then. At least they have each other, unlike my sister and me. Our paths led to very different places after we were separated at an early age. Oh well. She always was such a drag. As you can see, in the end, it's the strong one, not the lucky one or even the good one who survives. It's time to say good-bye now. This conversation is over. Watch your step!"

Chapter Twenty-Eight

Senora's demented laugh was the last sound I heard before hitting the water. I thought I had fallen face first onto an asphalt parking lot. I imagined myself skydiving without a parachute onto a glacier in Antarctica. There was only cold and screaming, cold and screaming. My arms and legs were flash frozen into useless dead weight. Even if I knew how to swim, my numb limbs were nothing more than anchors pulling me relentlessly down to the bottom of the lake. I was sinking. I recalled that the water temperature was somewhere between forty and fifty degrees, and if my memory was still at all accurate, I could expect to remain conscious between thirty and sixty minutes if I could keep my head above water. That was a huge if. In the best-case scenario, I could survive for one to three hours. I knew, however, that this was a worst-case situation. Soon, I would be dead. And the strangest thing of all was that I welcomed it. The farther I descended, the less I seemed to care about my present or my future. The icy fog in my brain was muddling my sense of time, place, and priority. I didn't know where June was or even if she was still alive.

But then another sound intruded into my consciousness. The grumbling of the boat's motor as Senora pulled away seemed to turn into the sweet noise that Beth and Ben used to make when they would put their faces into their bath water and blow bubbles, pretending to be pirates, whales, and mermaids engaging in deep sea adventurers. I fought to keep the picture of my beautiful children's faces in my mind as I accepted the fact it would be the last memory I would have on this Earth.

Then there were no more sounds; everything was eerily quiet. I remembered June had been with me and that she too was forced over the side of her boat. I hoped she would be rescued, but if, like me, she succumbed to the icy water, I hoped she would be waiting for me at the big wine garden in the sky. So this was it. In one final, lucid moment, I silently apologized to Hammond for ruining everything and asked for his forgiveness. I told him I loved him and waited for the end to come.

And now I couldn't even die in peace. A terrible pressure on my stomach and chest jolted me back from the brink, forcing me back into the horror of experiencing my last moments of life in agony. Something was squeezing me. Hallucinations were blending with reality. I was certain now that a slimy lake monster had wrapped its tentacles around my waist and was going to sweep me away to its lair. The pressure was getting stronger and stronger until I could no longer bear it. I was going to explode. No one would have to scatter my ashes at my funeral because tiny bits of Francesca would soon be dispersed throughout the water and air all around and above me. Something changed. I was being buoyed gently upward, back to the surface of the water. I could see a faint ray of light above me. It grew brighter and stronger until my head broke through the surface and I gasped in glorious pain as air entered my frozen lungs. As oxygen made its way to my brain, the first thing I comprehended was that I was miraculously still alive. The second thing I noticed was June's blond head bobbing barely above the water's surface, not far from my own. We drifted closer together, and in the faintest whisper, I heard June's voice.

"It's a boob."

After greedily sucking in some more air, my synapses began to fire again. My vocal chords crackled as they thawed and struggled to produce the words to verbalize the sight in front of my eyes. "Oh my God June, it is a boob! Quick grab on."

The useless paperback I had retrieved from my handbag and stuffed into the pocket of my sweatshirt at zero hour turned out to be the second water-activated raft I had bought for the twins at Jewel of the Bay last Friday. It had been activated in my pocket and borne me gently back to the surface. I could probably write a book on the symbolic irony of this whole situation.

Together we clung to the spongy, semi-pornographic, double-D, life-saving raft. Even though we were above water now, the frigid water was slowing our reactions, making us weaker by the second. It was becoming harder and harder to hold on. We had reached the point where it was impossible to speak through our chattering teeth. I looked at June's ghostly white face and ice-blue lips and assumed that my own face bore the same telltale characteristics of a person very close to her end. It was comforting to be together at least. We wrapped our arms around one another and pressed our bodies as close together as we could to share any tiny bit of warmth we still had in us. It was a little less scary knowing that I was not facing this horrible death alone.

My eyes closed heavily, and I was just drifting into oblivion when bright lights pricked at my eyelids and beckoned me to open them one more time. The lights were bright blue and red, blinding flashes piercing through the blackness, fireworks announcing our arrival to our heavenly hosts. This must be the end. Over the years, I had heard stories and read books recounting near-death experiences. Many people reported seeing a light before they passed, but I had always assumed it would be white light. Well, what did they know? I was dying in living color. June and I wouldn't have it any other way. The lights were getting closer and brighter. I entwined my fingers through June's and prepared myself for the end.

"Francie! June! Can you hear us? Francie! June!"

Using my last bit of energy, I cracked one eyelid open. The water was churning furiously around us, and now it seemed the entire universe was filled with the bright lights. And that's when the real miracle occurred. Detective Morgan's face filled my vision. He was leaning over the edge of his police boat, stretching, reaching, trying to drag June off the raft and out of the water. Clifton was there too, and the knock-off guy! I sure wish I could relay this final hallucination to my kids. They would be highly entertained.

"Grab my hand, Francie. Hold on, I've got you. You're going to be okay."

It took more effort than I had left at this point to realize I was not meeting my maker today. I was being rescued. June was alive. I was breathing and shivering so violently that I, too, must be among the living. The three men had managed to haul both of us into the rescue boat and wrap us in layers of blankets. As soon as everyone was safely seated, Morgan took the rescue vessel full speed ahead back to the mainland.

Chapter Twenty-Nine

It was Tuesday morning, I later was informed, when I finally opened my eyes. I was warm and dry, but I wasn't sure where I was or what new hell awaited me. Every inch of my body ached, and I thought about just closing my eyes and going back to sleep. At least it was quiet in my dreams. But something willed me into consciousness. I cautiously lifted my eyelids and what I saw was my amazingly handsome husband sitting in a chair pulled up right next to my bed. He had a gauze bandage wrapped around his head. His left arm was in a sling, and his right hand was holding tight to my own. He looked absolutely perfect.

"Hamm, you're alive! I knew it couldn't be true that Sirena or Senora or whatever her name is had killed you."

"I'm fine, darling. All that matters right now is that you're awake. How do you feel? Can I get you something? A glass of water?"

"I have everything I need right here. Don't let go of my hand please." My eyes were welling up, but these new tears were tears of relief and happiness. "Oh, honey, I can't believe I made it. I can't believe you're okay. Senora said she killed you."

"Oh, she tried all right. That's one bitter, twisted woman."

I squeezed my husband's hand, willing his warmth and strength to fill me and heal me. "Tell me what happened. I need to know."

"It can wait, Francie. Just rest now and get your strength back. I'm not going anywhere. You're safe now and I'll be right here."

"I don't think I can rest until I find out what happened." I didn't even want to blink. I was afraid I was hallucinating again and Hammond would be gone again if I did. "Please. Tell me."

Hamm took a deep breath, and looking steadily at me with his piercing blue eyes, began his tale.

"Sirena, or actually Senora, called me on my cell phone as I was heading back home Sunday morning. You can imagine how surprised I was to hear her voice. At first I thought something horrible must have happened to you."

Hamm squeezed my hand tighter before he continued. "She said she found my lighter and knew how upset I was about losing it. She said she could tell it was a very valuable piece and that I should stop by her shop to pick it up."

I had paid a lot for the gift, but I was sure Hamm had no idea of its monetary value. He never price-shopped, so I found it sweet to know the value he placed on the piece was sentimental.

"I didn't want to make an extra trip back to the island, but she was very insistent and I was passing the ferry dock when I got the call."

I thought back to the ferry trip that June and I had taken that same morning. It was a wonder we weren't on the same boat. He must have gone over before us because his car didn't stick out like a clown's red nose. He certainly would have noticed my old beater sitting in the near empty lot. I was sure that if we had run into each other then, it would have initiated an entirely different sequence of events.

Hamm went on. "She said it would make you very happy if you knew I went out of my way to get the lighter back. Once she read the inscription to me over the phone, I felt like I had no other choice."

I was getting sleepy again but I willed myself to stay alert so I could hear the rest of the story.

"Senora, who I still thought was Sirena, said she wanted to show me a captain's wheel necklace that you had been interested in when you visited her shop last Friday. She said she could order one and have it engraved with our boat's name in time for our anniversary." Hamm looked down at me sheepishly and said, "I took the bait. I made an exception since I know how much you love one-of-a-kind jewelry. I didn't want to waste any time getting home, but I made a quick decision to take the ferry over. I figured once I retrieved my lighter I would make a stop at the police station to tell Morgan that Sirena had found my lighter, and it was all a big mix-up. I thought he'd appreciate eliminating at least one of the leads he was following. I knew he had some suspicions about me when we talked at the party, but he's a fair man and I can't fault him for being thorough."

"Oh, Hamm, you have no idea how awful it was when I heard him saying you were a suspect not only in the fire but also for murder. I still can't believe that Sirena's own sister purposely led her into a trap and murdered her! What did she do to you when you showed up?"

"When I got to Sirena's shop, she was nowhere to be found. I waited a few minutes and was about to leave, angry that I had wasted my time, when a strange man with a ponytail grabbed me from behind and hit me over the head with something hard. I must have passed out because the next thing I knew I was tied up in a dark, fishy-smelling shack and left, I guess, to die. I had no idea what was going on or why I had been kidnapped. When I woke up, the guy was still there. He forced me to drink something. It didn't taste bad, but after that, I don't remember a thing. For the few seconds I was still conscious, all I could think of was you, and just prayed you were safe."

"Oh that's horrible! How did you escape?"

"I'd like to say I pulled a MacGyver and used a toothpick and some bubble gum to get myself out, but as it turned out, Jack Morgan figured out what Senora and this guy were up to and saved the day."

"How did he put it all together? I only remember bits and pieces of her crazy ranting, but I couldn't make much sense of it."

"We all owe a great deal to that guy June knows. Michael, you know the one with the German shepherd."

"Oh, of course, Michael and Gunner. Are they okay? The last time we saw Michael, he was being taken to the hospital. June and I found him near the breakwall and called an ambulance. We didn't know what happened to him, but there was blood and he was unconscious. We took his dog Gunner back to the condo with us, but by the time we got back after all the crazy things that happened, Gunner was gone. June called the hospital to check on Michael and he was also gone."

"Yes, he and Gunner are fine. Michael wouldn't admit it, but they're heroes. Michael left the hospital and tracked Gunner down at the condo. He was still a bit groggy from his head injury and the pain meds he was given, but he kept trying to put the pieces together. They were walking along the beach, taking the more scenic and private way back when everything fell into place. He knew something was wrong when he saw June's houseboat leaving the dock in the middle of the night. He tried to catch up to warn you and June. He knew June never took the boat out and became suspicious. He wasn't able to get to the boat in time to see who was driving, but when he reached the dock, he discovered Cliff in the water, barely hanging on to a dock post. He fished him out and contacted Morgan right away.

"Michael had been following a number of stories about a criminal investigation involving a murdered millionaire and a missing coin collection. He started with an article in the Chicago Tribune. Several other papers picked up on it. He became more interested when he read that the coins were being connected to various underworld collectors and investors. Later, he read a related story about counterfeit wholesale merchandise being funneled from Chicago and New York into the Midwest by these same crime rings."

"Now I remember Senora talking about Chicago and a black market business she was involved in. What else did you find out?"

"It turns out Michael had noticed activity at the old warehouse on Kelleys and began keeping tabs on a suspicious-looking guy who was coming and going quite frequently. The final piece of the puzzle fell into place when his dog became aggressive toward Sirena. Gunner had loved Sirena since the day she first snuck him one of her gourmet biscuits, but suddenly she couldn't get within five feet of him without causing the dog to growl."

"I didn't know that, or we would have been much more concerned when Gunner attacked Sirena's sweater. It makes sense now."

"Michael filled Morgan in on his suspicions, and the detective added it to the information he had been gathering and figured out the rest. When the police showed up to arrest Senora, she was not at her house or the store. She was probably already gone when she called me. That left her partner, the guy in black with the ponytail, Kenneth Overmayer. He was still hanging around, trying to decide what to do when Morgan caught up with him. After Morgan told him that Senora had left him to take the fall alone, and he would be charged with murder in the death of Sirena Divine, he caved. He made a deal with Morgan for leniency and took him to the shack where I was being held. Then he outlined to the authorities everything she was planning to do."

"Thank God. But wait! Where is June? Is Clifton okay? Did Senora get away? Everything is so fuzzy. I need to get up and get..." I stopped talking and looked around the room, realizing that I didn't recognize the space. "Where are we?"

Again, Hamm assured me that everything would be fine. He took my hand in both of his, raised it to his lips and gently kissed my fingertips.

"Everything is going to be fine, Fran. We are at the Firelands Medical Center. Apparently you don't remember the boat ride back, or the ambulance waiting at the marina? At any rate, you're alive. June is in the room next door. You both were in shock and fighting hypothermia, but with some rest, you'll be back to solving crimes together in no time."

I gave my man a weak smile. "I'm sorry I'm such a moron sometimes. I know I should have listened to you and kept my nose out of everyone's business, but I can't stand by and watch while my friends are in trouble."

"Well, it's not like any of this comes as a great surprise. There's never a dull moment around you, especially when you double the trouble and throw June into the mix. But I wouldn't change a single minute. Everyone knows you have a heart of gold."

"Tell me the rest of the story, Hamm. What happened to Cliff? Wasn't he in the boat when Morgan pulled June and me out of the lake? Things are still a little fuzzy."

"Cliff is fine. He was checked out by the doctors when you were brought in and after being watched for a few hours, they gave him the green light to leave. He decided to go back home. Turns out he's a pretty tough cookie in spite of his society boy attitude, but I think the real source of his pain now is the fact that Sirena is gone. He couldn't believe that he of all people didn't notice the change in her behavior after Senora had taken the place of her sister."

"Well, let's face it. He didn't know her all that well, and in his defense, none of us noticed any significant changes in her personality and certainly not in her appearance. Where is Senora now? Don't tell me she got away."

"She almost did. But Morgan and his team caught up with her at the warehouse. She was trying to salvage any of her counterfeit products and make sure there was nothing left that could incriminate her before she got out of town. They took her into custody and ran her name at the police station. That's when they found out she was wanted in Chicago for a whole array of crimes. Morgan called an old friend at his former precinct. He must have some pull over there because it was pretty amazing how quickly they were able to send two officers over to the island to arrest her. She's on her way back to the Windy City now where she will be in jail for a very long time."

"I hope she likes orange jumpsuits because she won't have many fashion options in prison."

Chapter Thirty

"Knock, knock. Is this a bad time?"

I reluctantly took my eyes off Hammond but was delighted when I saw Ruby and Roger Burns standing in the doorway with a huge bouquet of daisies and irises and the biggest "Get Well" helium balloon I had ever seen.

"We came as soon as we heard what happened." Ruby stepped closer and put the cheery gifts on the bedside table.

"Come on in. I'm so happy to see you both! I'm just glad this nightmare is over, and no one else was seriously hurt."

Roger entered the room a step behind his wife. His typical gregarious demeanor was gone. He looked solemn and serious standing now beside my bed.

"What's wrong, Roger? Is there something else? I don't think I can take any more bad news."

"I feel terrible about this whole thing, Francie. So much of this disaster could have been avoided if I had handled things differently. I feel like I owe you all an apology."

I was confused. "Roger, you have nothing to feel guilty about. You and Ruby were victims of that horrible Senora and her shady mob friends. June and I were responsible for our own trouble. We just wanted to help, but obviously we should have left the investigation to the professionals."

"Well, as you're probably aware by now, I got myself wrapped up in some of those crooks' shady deals and couldn't figure out how to separate myself from them without hurting the people I love most."

"Oh Roger, I'm sure it was all a big misunderstanding. Those people were horrible."

"Yes, they were, and I should have known better than to think I could make a single deal with them then walk away without consequences. About a year ago, I was approached by Kenneth Overmayer with a deal that seemed too good to be true, and of course it was. He showed me some samples of very popular designer merchandise with pricing far below anything I'd ever seen anywhere else. He said he bought the goods in bulk and eliminated the middlemen. He told me he wanted to pass the savings along to me and other area retailers, hoping to build up his sales and transport business. He produced very legitimate-looking credentials and references, so I agreed because I thought Ruby's customers would love the products and we could make a nice profit. It seemed like a win-win situation, but it turned out to be just the opposite."

Roger shifted uncomfortably from foot to foot, and wiped his palms on the front of his shirt. Ruby put a steady hand on Roger's shoulder for support but didn't speak. Finally, he cleared his throat and continued.

"I placed the first order with Overmayer and Ruby couldn't keep the stuff on the shelves. It wasn't until I had bought and sold three large shipments that he informed me that fifty percent of the merchandise I was selling to my customers was counterfeit. He said it was so good that the average consumer would never know, but if I didn't continue buying his knock-offs, he would inform the authorities and I would be forced out of business. Since my signature was on all the orders, I felt I had no choice but to continue dealing with him."

I was thinking that June and I were not average consumers, which is why we were able to spot the knock-offs. Hamm turned to Roger and asked, "Roger, did this man ever threaten you or your family? Lawyer mode had kicked in."

"I'm embarrassed to say that he did. I don't know why I didn't go to the police right away, but after a while, I felt like I was every bit as guilty as he was. He said if I tried to turn him in, I would end up in jail as an accomplice, and worse yet, if I didn't go along with all his expansion plans, he would make sure I would regret it. When I hesitated, he made good on that promise, and after the fire, things spiraled downward. He made sure I understood that if I didn't do whatever he told me, my wife would end up like the person in the attic."

Roger's voice was hoarse with emotion. Ruby's eyes were welling up with tears. "My God! Poor Sirena! I'll never be able to forgive myself for what happened to her."

"You had no way of knowing what Senora had planned for her sister." Hamm was trying valiantly to help ease Roger's guilt. "Overmayer didn't even know about that, but once Senora told him what she had done, he too was blackmailed into helping her carry out her scheme. It doesn't by any means excuse his actions." Hamm squeezed my hand as he continued. "He was no match for my Francie, though."

I smiled weakly. My head ached and I felt myself losing focus. "Can I just have a hug?" It was all I had left in me to say.

Ruby and Roger approached my bed. Ruby bent over and brushed a light kiss on my forehead, while Roger awkwardly patted the hand that Hamm was not still clutching. "I'm glad that you girls are going to be okay."

"Stop by the store as soon as you're up and about," Ruby added as the couple took their leave. "I have something special waiting for you and June. Hamm, take good care of that girl. She's one in a million."

"Don't you worry about that. I might stop by myself and buy something pretty for my wonderful wife."

"Oh, that's lovely..." I breathed a sigh of relief as my eyes shut and I drifted off into the most peaceful sleep I can ever remember.

Chapter ThirtyOne

I LOOKED TO THE RIGHT of my lawn chair toward June and held my frozen margarita up toward hers in a toast. "Cheers!" we exclaimed in unison.

Our one-of-a-kind hand-etched glasses, courtesy of Ruby and Roger Burns, clinked with satisfaction, and the tart lime flavor of our drinks brought smiles to our faces. The frightful events of the last few days were behind us. We had survived. Life was once again in our control. We were being pampered and waited on by the two handsome men standing on the back deck of the condo in front of the shiny, stainless steel barbecue grill. We sat back, content to be in the shade, and listened as Hamm and Morgan debated the advantages and disadvantages of using gas versus coal for grilling the perfect hamburger. Since the impressive gas grill belonged to Hamm, and since we were after all, at the Egge homestead, Jack deferred to the chef. He walked across the deck to the lawn where June and I lounged in my new gravity chairs enjoying the peaceful view of the lake we all loved so well. There was not a cloud in the sky or a wave on the water.

I had some lingering bruises and scrapes, but overall I was fine. June had recovered quickly, just like she did everything else. Her hair was basic blond now since she hadn't had time to get to the salon. She wore no makeup, which gave her a sweet, vulnerable look. Her toenails, however, were painted an interesting olive green and her fingernails were pimento red. It worked on her. Jack stopped behind June's chair and placed his hands on her shoulders, kneading his fingers along the muscles in her neck with a touch that suggested they were more than just friends. If I had blinked, I would have missed the discreet kiss he planted behind her ear. He whispered something before casually heading back to the deck. From the cooler he retrieved a Bud Lite, pulled back the tab, and raised the can to his lips with a very satisfied expression on his face. June looked my way and winked.

"You girls are lucky you're both so cute," Jack announced. "I thought you'd like to know that you don't need to worry about those interesting IOUs you've been leaving around town. The kayak and the tandem bike are back with their rightful owners, and speaking of the owners, both of them waived all the rental charges. They both were impressed with your honesty and your creativity. Business is booming since pictures of the bike and kayak appeared on Facebook, and to top it all off, Francie and June, you are local celebrities and even have a Twitter following, whatever that is! The bike shop owner wants to know if he can use a picture of the two of you on the tandem bike in a new ad for his business."

Hamm looked at me over the rim of his glass and we exchanged a look that carried with it an entire unspoken conversation.

Smiling, I said, "Of course he can use our photo—for a fee of course!" It felt good to have a light-hearted conversation again. I sipped my frozen drink and looked at these three people: the love of my life, the friend who was part of my soul, and the newcomer who bore great future potential. I planned to be around for many more years so I could enjoy everything that life threw our way.

"Who wants cheese on their burger?"

"Duh! What kind of a question is that?" I retorted.

"Yeah," June agreed. "You should be asking what kind of cheese. And make it a double!"

We all laughed. This was an extra cheese event if ever there was one.

From inside, the voice of Clifton Sterling drifted out from the television, which had been tuned to the WLKE evening news.

"Tonight I bring you an exclusive breaking news report."

It doesn't get any better than this.